"Take a risk, Mari."

Her gaze leaped to meet his. Was he a mind reader?

"All right," she whispered. "But I can't guarantee anything. And I want to take things slowly...test out the waters." *See what kind of effect our being seen together has on our family and friends,* she added privately. She grimaced at her thought, realizing Marc was right to suggest she considered everyone else before she did herself.

He pulled her closer. He didn't say anything, but she found herself wondering if he thought the same thing she did. They'd learned fifteen years ago that life was tenuous. People who thought happiness was guaranteed, that security was a certainty, were living in a dream.

But did that mean the dream wasn't worth seeking?

Dear Reader,

I hope you will enjoy this romance of love lost and reclaimed set against the emotional backdrop of torn loyalties and the struggle to find meaning in the aftermath of tragedy. Marc and Mari's story is very personal to me, but I believe it will strike a chord in any reader who believes, as I do, that love and hope can truly conquer all, if given a chance.

I would like to thank my agent, Laura Bradford, for believing in this story, and Susan Litman, my editor, for being patient with me as I have attempted to learn the art of writing category romance. As always, I'm grateful to my husband for his unfailing support and the inspiration I get from him in so many different ways.

Beth Kery

THE HOMETOWN HERO RETURNS

BETH KERY

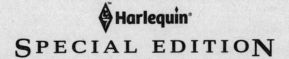

Harlequin®

SPECIAL EDITION

Recycling programs
for this product may
not exist in your area.

ISBN-13: 978-0-373-65594-6

THE HOMETOWN HERO RETURNS

This edition published by arrangement with Harlequin Books S.A.

For questions and comments about the quality of this book please contact us at Customer_eCare@Harlequin.ca.

www.eHarlequin.com

Printed in U.S.A.

Recent books by Beth Kery

Special Edition

The Hometown Hero Returns #2112

BETH KERY

holds a doctorate degree in the behavioral sciences and enjoys incorporating what she's learned about human nature into her stories. To date, she has published more than a dozen novels and short stories and writes in multiple genres, always with the overarching theme of passionate, emotional romance. To find out about upcoming books in the Harbor Town series, visit Beth at her website at www.BethKery.com or join her for a chat at her reader group, www.groups.yahoo.com/group/BethKery.

Prologue

He'd followed her for three blocks, undecided whether he would call out or just fade back into the shadows of their mutual memories. The weight of the past had frozen his vocal cords, but the sight of her graceful figure drew him like a magnet.

He repeatedly told himself there was no reason for so much trepidation. There was nothing between Mari and him now. The common ground they once shared was shadowed by his shame for his father's actions as well as the bitterness he felt toward Mari for refusing to see or speak to him for half a lifetime.

He nearly did a complete turnabout in the revolving doors of the Palmer House Hotel, telling himself it would be best to just walk away. But at the last second, impulse drove him to speak her name.

"Marianna."

She glanced around.

Mari's eyes—God, he'd forgotten their power. The

sounds in the bustling, luxurious hotel lobby faded as the color washed out of her cheeks. He felt a stab of regret. It'd been the sight of her breathtaking face that'd compelled him to pull up short and call her name.

For a few seconds, they remained motionless. The single word he'd uttered had been the first they'd shared since they'd both lost loved ones in one cruel swipe of fate's hand.

"Marc," Mari mouthed.

"I was at your performance and I followed you," he explained rapidly. When she continued to stare at him, her expression rigid with shock, he realized how strange that sounded. "I just wanted to say…you were wonderful."

She set down her cello case and straightened, seeming to gather herself. Her small smile seemed to give him permission to step closer. "Since when does Marc Kavanaugh listen to anything but rock music?"

"Give me some credit, Mari. A lot can change in fifteen years."

"I'll grant you that," she replied softly.

He couldn't stop himself from devouring the sight that had been ripped away from him so long ago. She wore the black dress that was standard apparel for a symphony member. The garment was simple and elegant, but it couldn't hide the fact that womanhood had added some curves to Mari's slender form.

In all the right places, Marc acknowledged as his gaze lingered for two heartbeats on her full breasts. He glanced down at her hands and noticed she was twisting them together, betraying her nerves. Mari was a cellist—a brilliant one. She had the hands of musician—sensitive and elegant. Even though she'd been young and inexperienced when they'd been together so long ago, she'd had a magical touch on his appreciative skin.

"Look at you. Marianna Itani, all grown up."

"You, too."

Maybe it was his imagination, but her lowered glance seemed almost as hungry as his inspection of her had been.

She returned his smile when she looked into his eyes. "Every inch the newly elected Cook County State's Attorney."

"How did you know about that?"

She shrugged. "I read about it. I wasn't surprised. It was a foregone conclusion you'd excel at whatever you did. You always got what you wanted, once you made up your mind about it." She swallowed and glanced away. "I was sorry to hear about your divorce."

He raised an eyebrow. "I'm sure that didn't make any headlines. How *did* you know about that?"

She looked uncomfortable. "I still have a few contacts in Harbor Town. I keep in touch."

Not with me though, Mari. Fifteen years of silence. Marc banished the flash of frustration, knowing how fruitless the emotion was.

"Right." He nodded, understanding dawning. "I wouldn't be surprised if Walt Edelmann over at the Shop and Save was the first person to know about my divorce outside of Sandra and myself. It's almost supernatural the way that man acquires gossip."

Her radiant smile made a dull ache expand in his chest. "Do you think Walt still works at the Shop and Save?"

"I know he does. I don't go back to Harbor Town often, but, when I do, I always see Walt. He's a standard fixture. He and my mother chat almost every day, which is code for exchanging juicy news."

Her glance ricocheted off him at the mention of his mother. The light from the lobby chandeliers made the dark gold highlights in her brown hair gleam when she lowered her head. "Well...you know how small towns are."

"Yeah, I do," he replied gruffly.

She stirred beneath his stare. The moment wasn't as awkward as it was tense. Charged. He waited, wondering what she would say. He was having trouble finding words himself. He and Mari were almost strangers to each other now. It was odd, the paradox of connection and distance he felt with this woman, as though they each stood on the opposite side of a great chasm of grief, joined only by a thin, ephemeral thread.

Still, that cord was strong enough that it had tugged at him this afternoon when he'd seen the newspaper article about the San Francisco Orchestra playing at Symphony Hall; it had made him ask his administrative assistant to buy him a ticket to the performance. It had fueled his impulsive decision to follow Mari to her hotel.

He nodded in the direction of a crowded lounge. "Can I buy you a drink?"

She hesitated. He was sure she was going to say it wasn't a good idea. He might have agreed with her five minutes ago, before he'd been stunned by the visceral impact of standing so close to her...of seeing her face.

"I have a suite. There's a separate room where we could have a drink and talk. I mean...if you'd like," she added when he didn't immediately respond.

Seeing the slight tremble in her lush lips had mesmerized him.

He blinked, wondering if he was seeing things he wanted to see, not reality. In eyes that reminded him of rare cognac, he saw the glow of desire, a heat that hadn't been entirely stamped out by the weight of tragedy.

"That sounds like a great idea."

She nodded, but neither of them moved. The bond

he'd shared with Mari since they'd been sunburned, carefree teenagers in Harbor Town—a bond formed by love and battered by grief—chose that moment to recall its strength and coil tight.

He stepped forward at the same moment she came toward him and enfolded her in his arms. A convulsion of emotion shook her body.

"Shh." His hand found its way into her smooth, soft hair. He fisted a handful and lifted it to his nose. Her scent filled his head. Desire roared in his blood.

"Mari," he whispered.

He pressed his mouth to her brow, her eyelid and cheek. He felt her go still in his arms when he kissed the corner of her mouth. She turned her head slowly, her lips brushing against his. Their breaths mingled. A powerful need surged up in him, its primal quality shocking him. He possessively covered her mouth.

When he lifted his head a moment later, she was panting softly through well-kissed lips.

"Lead the way, Mari."

"I can think of a thousand reasons we shouldn't do this," she whispered.

"I can only think of you."

She put her hand in his and they headed toward the elevators that led to the rooms.

Chapter One

Five weeks later

Mari understood, for the first time in her life, the full meaning of the word *bittersweet* when she returned to Harbor Town after nearly fifteen years. The feeling strengthened when she left the empty office complex on the north end of town and saw Lake Michigan shimmering through the trees.

"We're not far from Silver Dune Bay here, are we?" she asked Eric Reyes as he paused beside her. She waved goodbye to Marilyn Jordan, the real estate agent who had just shown them the commercial property.

"Fancy a swim, do you? It's hot enough for one, that's for sure." His grin faded. "Mari? Are you okay? You're very pale."

She brushed a tendril of hair off her sweaty brow and steadied herself by leaning against the wall of the building. She swallowed thickly, trying to calm the nausea swelling in her belly.

"I'm fine. I think I caught a bug. The guy who sat next to me on the plane was coughing nonstop for the whole trip."

Eric studied her through narrowed eyes. Mari was suddenly reminded that her friend was a doctor, a very gifted one by all accounts.

"It's nothing, Eric," she assured him. "It comes and goes. I'm sure this heat isn't helping matters any."

She stepped away from the wall, willing her queasiness to ease. She didn't have time for illness. This was a trip she'd needed to make for a long time, and she'd planned to complete her mission in a quick and dirty fashion. Because of her impulsiveness with Marc Kavanaugh five weeks ago, her desire to take care of business and get out of Harbor Town as soon as possible only intensified by the hour.

She forced a smile and walked with Eric toward his sedan.

"Were you one of the daredevils who used to jump off Silver Dune? It's got to be a forty-foot drop to the bay," she reflected as Eric unlocked the passenger door of his car. In her mind's eye, she pictured her summertime best friend Colleen Kavanaugh leaping off the tall dune without a backward glance, her long blond hair streaming out behind her like a golden cape.

Mari had always been a little in awe of the Kavanaughs' fearlessness. All the children had seemed to possess that indefinable, elusive quality that Mari thought of as American royalty—the golden, effortless beauty, the easy confidence and quick smile, the love of a dare, a fierce temper and an even fiercer loyalty to those they loved.

"It's fifty feet, actually," Eric replied once she was

seated in the car. He shut her door and came around to
the driver's side. After he flipped the ignition, he immediately turned the air conditioning on high to cool
the stifling interior. "And yeah, I took the leap plenty
of times in my day."

Took the leap.

Mari had only had the nerve to leap once in her life.
She still could see Marc staring down at her, his mouth
quirked in a sexy, little smile even as the rest of his
features were softened in compassion for her fear.

Stop thinking so much, Mari. Just jump.

She *had* jumped, back when she was eighteen years
old. It'd been the summer her parents had been killed.

Foolishness had caused her to take a similar reckless
leap five weeks ago in Chicago. As a thirty-three-year-
old woman, Mari hardly had the excuse of a girlhood
infatuation any longer, yet something fluttered in her
belly as she clearly recalled Marc pinning her with the
blazing blue eyes as he fused their flesh. She heard his
desire-roughened voice in her ear.

I've waited for this for fifteen years, Mari.

She clenched her eyelids shut and placed her hand on
her stomach, not to soothe her nausea this time, but to
calm the thrill of excitement and wonder the memory
evoked. When she opened her eyes, she saw Eric's curious glance raking over her.

"So are you going to keep me in suspense or what?"
he asked as he pulled onto Route 6.

"What do you mean?" she asked warily, still under
the influence of the carnal memory.

Eric gave her a bewildered glance. "I'm wondering
what you think of the property, Mari."

"Oh!" She laughed in relief. For a second there, she'd
thought those physician's eyes of his had x-rayed straight
into her skull and read her thoughts. "I *do* like the office

space. Very much. It's in a private area, and I love all the sunlight. It's nice that it's so close to the woods and the lake. There's plenty of room for The Family Center to grow as we get new funding and programs. Thank you so much for doing all the preliminary groundwork before I got here, Eric. You and Natalie have done a hundred times more than I'd expected."

"It wasn't that much, especially with all the research and ideas you sent us. Plus, you'd already compiled most of the paperwork for the state."

"Most people will think I'm nuts for doing this—a cello player opening up a facility for victims of substance abuse," she muttered.

Eric's dark brows quirked upward. "Good thing the Reyes aren't *most people* then."

Mari smiled. Of course the Reyes weren't most people. Eric and Natalie had been just as impacted by the effects of substance abuse as Mari and her brother, Ryan, had.

And the Kavanaughs...

It'd been fifteen years since a drunk Derry Kavanaugh, Marc's father, had gotten behind the wheel of his car. Marc's father had caused a three-way crash that night, killing himself, both of Mari's parents and Eric's mother. The accident had left Eric's sister, Natalie, scarred—damage both physical and psychological.

This was the old wound that Mari had felt compelled to return to Harbor Town and try to heal. Not just for herself or Eric or Natalie or Marc, but for anyone who had ever been impacted by the devastating effects of substance abuse.

Eric grabbed her hand as he drove. "Nat and I are right here in Harbor Town, and we're one hundred percent behind you on this. Are you *sure* you don't need any of the money from the lawsuit? Do you really think it was the best idea to transfer all of it over to a trust for The Family Center?"

"Of course I'm sure. You know I've planned to start this project with money from the lawsuit for years now. I never could touch that fund for anything else. It just seemed like—" she paused, trying to find the right words "—that money was meant for something bigger than me. I just haven't had the time to get things moving until now. Besides, I'm selling the house on Sycamore Avenue. That'll give Ryan and me a nice nest egg."

She glanced out the window at the rows of perfectly maintained lakeside cottages. Each and every one looked to be occupied with vacationers. The population of Harbor Town swelled in the summer months.

She smiled wistfully as she watched a little girl with a dark ponytail run around the corner of a house. She'd sported a pink bikini and an inflatable green dragon around her waist.

"I'm not sure I'll ever have the time I need to do what needs to be done," she murmured.

Eric wiggled her hand in his before he let go. "You know what I think you need? I think you need a little fun and relaxation, Harbor Town-style."

"What did you have in mind?"

"The Fourth of July festivities, of course. Don't tell me you've forgotten the downtown parade."

Mari laughed warily. "How could I forget such a spectacle?"

"Let's go have a peek, get an ice cream, goof off. There's plenty of time later to sit down and talk about the plans for The Family Center."

"Eric…" Mari hesitated, hating the idea of being seen in such a public place. Marc had mentioned five weeks ago that he rarely returned to Harbor Town, but she knew that his sister, Colleen, still lived here, as did their mother, Brigit. At the thought of running into either of them—especially Brigit—dread rose.

"Mari," Eric said gently. "You have nothing to be ashamed of. Isn't that one of the reasons you wanted to start up The Family Center, to get past the pain of our history, to make something positive come of it? You can't do that by hiding in your house the whole time you're here."

Her eyes felt moist as she stared blankly out the window. Eric was right. Surely it was part of her own healing to remember not just the bitterness but the sweetness associated with the quaint lakeside community.

"All right," she replied softly. "Let's go to the parade."

Mari stood next to Eric on the curb of Main Street. A boisterous crowd of locals, vacationers and day-trippers surrounded them. A trombone blared off-key, startling her. She glanced up at Eric, and they shared a smile.

A huge sailboat float, surrounded by the smiling, waving men and women of the Arab-American Business Council, followed the marching band. Harbor Town was one of many quaint Michigan towns that lined the lakeshore, drawing vacationers from Detroit and Chicago and everywhere in between. A small population of Arab-Americans had settled in many lakeside communities over the past several decades. Harbor Town was often held up as a banner example of how a minority group could not only blend with a community, but enrich and improve it. Her parents had belonged to a Lebanese faction of eastern orthodox Christianity—the Maronites. Despite the minority status of their religion among Arab-Americans, Kassim and Shada Itani had taken comfort in having others around who shared so many common cultural elements.

"Oh, look! It's Alex Kouri," Mari exclaimed as a distinguished man in his sixties marched past. His eyes widened incredulously as his gaze landed on her, and he waved and mouthed her name.

Mr. Kouri had been one of her father's closest friends. Both of them had been Detroit-based businessmen who had brought their families to Harbor Town for summer vacations. Mr. Kouri and her father would frequently drive back and forth together from Harbor Town to Dearborn, Michigan, on Friday and Sunday evenings, leaving their families to idle away the hot, summer weekdays while they worked at their corporate jobs.

Mari noticed how gray Mr. Kouri's hair had become. That's how her father would have looked, had he lived.

She saw a woman standing at the curb, her rapt attention on Mari and Eric, not on the parade. *Still as nosey as ever,* Mari thought with a flash of irritation, recognizing Esther Fontel, the old neighbor from Sycamore Avenue. The woman had once ratted her out to her parents when she observed Mari sneaking out her bedroom window and down the trusty old elm tree to join Marc on his motorcycle one hot summer night. Mari still recalled how angry her father had been, the hurt and the disappointment on her mother's face.

Until she'd turned fifteen, Mari hadn't fully understood the impact that her parents' ethnicity and religious views would have on her. Her brother had dated and enjoyed any number of summertime, teenage dalliances in Harbor Town. When Mari became a young woman, however, she'd learned firsthand that Ryan and she would not be treated the same when it came to dating. Especially when it came to Marc Kavanaugh.

Marc and Ryan had been close friends since they were both ten years old. Her parents had actually both been very fond of Marc, and he was a regular visitor in the Itani vacation home.

But the summer Mari had turned fifteen, everything had changed—and Marc Kavanaugh had quickly moved to the top of her parents' list of undesirable dating partners for Mari.

Mrs. Fontel looked pointedly across the street, and Mari followed her gaze. She stared, shock vibrating her consciousness. Two tall, good-looking men with healthy, golden tans and dark blond hair stood in the crowd. Her gaze stuck on the one with the short, wavy hair. He had a little girl perched on his shoulders.

He looked just as good in shorts and a T-shirt that skimmed his lean, muscular torso as he had in the gray suit he'd worn in Chicago, Mari thought dazedly.

Her glance flickered to the right of Liam and Marc, and Brigit Kavanaugh's furious glare struck her like a slap to the face from an ice cold hand. Marc's stare was fiercer, though. It seemed to bore right through her across the span of Main Street.

It felt like someone had reached inside her and twisted her intestines. He'd said he only returned to Harbor Town a few times a year, she thought wildly. What were the chances he'd be here for the same handful of days she was?

She shivered despite the heat. It was Independence Day. Tomorrow would be the anniversary of the crash. Perhaps the Kavanaughs had gathered to visit Derry Kavanaugh's grave. Why hadn't she considered that possibility?

She jerked her gaze back to the parade, making no sense of the flashing, moving, colorful scene before her eyes, still highly aware of him watching her. He'd always been able to melt her with those blue eyes. She could only imagine the effect they had on the people he'd cross-examined in the courtroom.

Mari had certainly felt the power of his stare during that night in Chicago.

He must be furious at her for not showing up at their agreed-upon lunch, for not returning his calls…especially after what had occurred between them in that hotel room.

"Well, if it isn't Mari Itani," Liam Kavanaugh drawled under his breath.

Marc followed Liam's gaze, too surprised by his brother's statement to comment at first. He immediately found Mari in the crowd. She wore her long hair up and a casual, yellow dress that tied beneath her full breasts in a bow. The garment set off Mari's flawless, glowing skin to perfection. Not to mention what that innocent-seeming ribbon did to highlight the fullness of her curves.

"Mari Itani?" Marc's sister Colleen asked incredulously from behind him. "Where?"

"Stop pointing, Liam," Brigit Kavanaugh scolded when Liam tried to show his sister where Mari stood.

"Did you know she was back, Mom?" Marc asked sharply.

"I knew it. She's just here to get the house in order before it goes on the market. Can't believe she and Ryan have waited this long to sell it, but obviously they haven't been hurting for money," Brigit replied bitterly.

"Mommy, can we follow the parade down the street? I want to see Brendan again. He looked so funny," Marc's niece, Jenny, begged from her perch on his shoulders. Marc's nephew, Brendan, had marched in the parade as part of the Harbor Town Swim and Dive Club.

Colleen laughed and reached up for her six-year-old daughter. Marc bent his knees to make the transfer easier.

"Aren't you coming, Uncle Marc?" Jenny asked, tugging on his hand once her feet were firmly on the ground.

"I'll stay here and keep Grandma company. Tell us if Brendan trips or anything," Marc replied.

Jenny grinned broadly at the prospect and yanked her mother down the sidewalk.

Liam chuckled. "How come sisters always want to see their brothers humiliated?"

"Probably because brothers make it their mission to ignore their sisters," Marc muttered, his gaze again fixed on the vision in yellow across the street.

"It looks like Mari grew up real nice," Liam murmured as he rubbed his goatee speculatively. Liam wore sunglasses, but Marc sensed the appreciative gleam in his brother's eyes as he studied Mari. When he saw Marc's glare, Liam just raised his eyebrows in a playful expression that said loud and clear, *so sue me for noticing the obvious.*

He felt like he was still recovering from a sucker punch to the gut.

At first, he'd had the wild thought that her presence in Harbor Town was somehow related to what had happened in that hotel room in Chicago. When he saw how Mari made a point of avoiding his gaze, though, he wondered.

"Is Ryan with her?" Marc asked slowly, not liking the idea of Mari's insolent brother residing down the street from his mom, even if it was just for a few nights. Ryan Itani's behavior during the lawsuit hearings stood out as one of the worst in a collection of bad memories from that time of his life.

"No. Ryan's still in the Air Force, doing a tour of duty

in Afghanistan. I just heard Mari was here to sell the house, and I saw the car in the driveway, so I guess it's true. It's none of my business. I'm just relieved they're finally selling. That house has been a blight on Sycamore Avenue for fifteen years now. Mari and Ryan wouldn't even rent it out to vacationers."

"You'd have just complained if they'd rented it out to vacationers, Ma. Besides, Joe Brown keeps the place in good shape."

Liam paused when Brigit shot him an annoyed glance. Marc smirked at his brother. *You walked right into that trap, sucker.* Liam should have known better than to say something *reasonable* when it came to the topic of the Itanis. Hadn't they learned years ago that when it came to matters of grief and loss, logic went the way of friendship, compassion…love?

Straight to hell, in other words.

"Who's the guy with Mari?" Liam asked once their view was no longer obscured.

Marc froze. He'd been so focused on Mari he hadn't noticed the tall, good-looking man standing next to her.

Brigit sniffed at Liam's question.

"That's Eric Reyes. He's a doctor now. I'm sure Mari and him have plenty to talk about. Gloat over, more likely. I think I'll go and catch up with Colleen. There's nothing left to see here," Brigit said before she departed in a huff.

So *that* was Eric Reyes. The seething, skinny kid he recalled from the court battle for his father's estate had grown into a formidable-looking man. Had his mother said *doctor?* Reyes must have used the money he'd received in the lawsuit to send himself to medical school.

Fury burned in his chest. Not about the lawsuit. He

was a state's attorney, after all, a victim's advocate first and foremost. Marc had long ago come to terms with the fact that in catastrophes like the one his father had caused, the victims' damages weren't likely to be covered merely by insurance. A good portion of his father's personal assets had been ordered liquidated and disbursed to the Itani and Reyes families.

He'd never been able to make his mother see things as he did. Feeling as if she and her children were being punished for Derry's crime, Brigit had been bewildered and hurt by the other families' legal actions. Brigit had needed to sell the family home in Chicago and relocate to the summer house in Harbor Town. She'd been forced to pay a good portion of a lifetime's savings, including her children's college funds, in order to legally amend for her husband's actions.

The crash had meant crushing loss and grief. The lawsuits had built walls of betrayal and fury between the families involved.

Mari had never actively taken part in the proceedings. Her aunt and older brother had kept her protected in Chicago following her parents' deaths. She'd been young at the time—only eighteen. As he studied Mari's averted profile, Marc wondered for the hundred thousandth time what she thought of the whole affair, what she'd thought of him all these years. The topic had never come up during that intense, impulsive night in Chicago.

They'd been too involved in other things.

He grimaced at the thought. He couldn't help but feel the stark symbolism of having shared something so intimate with Mari only to now be standing on opposite sides of a Harbor Town street.

Reyes put his arm around Mari's shoulder and stroked skin that Marc knew from experience was as soft and smooth as a new flower petal.

It made sense, Mari together with Reyes. Blood was thicker than water, but shared, spilled blood was perhaps even more binding. Isn't that what they said about soldiers who watched each other's backs in wartime? They'd do favors for each other that they might refuse to do for a family member.

I can't compete with that, he thought darkly.

He wasn't sure he wanted to. Not after Mari had made a point of abandoning him following their soul-searing reunion.

"Are you going to talk to her?" Liam prodded.

He twisted his mouth into a frown. "Something tells me she doesn't want to have anything to do with me."

Liam's eyebrows shot up. He opened his mouth to say something, but when Marc turned a grim face to him, he closed it again.

By the time Marc entered Jake's Place accompanied by Colleen and Liam at ten that night, Colleen had commented on his bad mood. Marc had gone from preoccupied to morose as the day had progressed. He'd convinced himself that Mari was right to avoid him. Their impulsive tryst in Chicago had been a mistake, some kind of residual, emotional backfire from their charged history together as kids.

He'd just gotten a divorce eighteen months ago. Hadn't he made a firm pact with himself that he wasn't going to consider any serious relationships for quite some time, anyway?

No sooner had they stepped into Jake's loud, crowded, front room when Marc saw her. She sat in a booth across from Eric Reyes, laughing at something he'd just said. Even though Marc had decided just seconds ago that Mari and he were best separated by two thirds of a continent, his feet seemed to disagree with his brain.

This had nothing to do with logic.

He plunged through the crowd, ignoring Colleen's shouted question. His entire awareness had narrowed down to a single, precise focus.

Mari's eyes widened in surprise when he strode up to the booth.

"Let's dance, Mari."

Chapter Two

Mari stared mutely up at Marc. The man's full impact struck her just as powerfully as it had when he'd unexpectedly tracked her down in Chicago.

God, he'd turned into a beautiful man.

His once-light hair had darkened to a burnished gold. He wore it short now, but the conservative style couldn't suppress the natural wave. Whiskers shadowed his jaw. He looked just as good in a suit and tie as he did in the casual white button-down shirt and jeans he wore at present, but Mari knew which outfit Marc preferred. The wildness of the Kavanaugh spirit could never be disguised by the packaging of refined clothing.

He was still as lean as he'd been at twenty-one, but he'd gained some muscle in his chest and shoulders. She dragged her eyes off the tempting sight of his strong thighs and narrow hips encased in faded, extremely well-fitting denims and met his stare.

He looked good enough to eat—*and* furious. His

eyes glittered like blue flames in his tanned face. Just before he walked up to the booth, she'd been telling Eric she was feeling exhausted after their busy day. Yet one look at Marc, and her blood was pumping madly in her veins, washing away every hint of fatigue.

"Uh, sure," she replied. She couldn't think of a good reason to refuse a dance without sounding rude or highlighting the significance of the encounter. If she agreed, surely people would just assume it was a casual dance between two old sweethearts.

Neither she nor Marc spoke as he led her to the edge of the crowded dance floor. The cover band was playing an '80s classic with a good beat. Marc put his arm around her waist, and they began to move as naturally as if their last dance had been yesterday.

Mari kept her gaze averted from his face, but she was hyperaware of every point of contact of their bodies, how well they fit one another…how perfectly they moved together.

She'd thought something similar five weeks ago when they'd finally made love.

Heat flooded her cheeks at the memory. So much emotional baggage separated them. Why was it, then, that being in his arms felt so right—so natural?

She recalled watching him dress as morning sunlight had peeked around the heavy draperies in the Palmer House hotel room. Marc needed to get back to his condo to shower and then rush to a meeting, but they'd already agreed to have lunch.

And dinner.

From the bed, Mari was admiring the shape of his long legs as he stepped into his pants when he caught her staring. He paused and they shared a smile that brought to mind the night spent in each other's arms, the nearly unbearable pleasure of touching each other, of complete communion after so long and after so much.

Marc's cell phone rang, breaking their stare. He ignored it, but after a pause, it started ringing again.

"Maybe you should answer," she murmured with a smile. "Sounds important."

Gleaming with heat, his eyes remained fixed on her, while he reached for the phone.

"Hey, Mom," he said.

It'd been like a bucket of ice water had been tossed in her face.

Everything had come back—all the anguish, all the grief, all the memories of why they'd been ripped apart so long ago.

Ryan had once told her Brigit Kavanaugh had confronted him after a day in court. "Don't you understand that I lost my husband in that accident? I'm mourning just like you are. Why are you trying to punish me further by taking everything away from my children? Have you no pity?" Brigit had tearfully asked Ryan.

The memory of her brother's encounter always made Mari recoil in pain. She hadn't been around during the court proceedings, but distance hadn't been able to diminish her knowledge of all the hurt between the Kavanaughs and the Itanis.

That's why, after Marc had left the hotel room, she'd packed her bags and caught the first flight she could back to San Francisco. Some things just weren't meant to be.

Even if they did feel so right.

Their thighs, hips and bellies slid together provocatively as they danced. Every once in a while, the tips of her breasts would brush his ribs. Her nipples felt achy, overly sensitive. It excited her, their furtive, subtle, rhythmic caresses. A strange brew of emotions simmered inside her—nervousness, uncertainty, longing…

Arousal.

She stared over Marc's shoulder, not really seeing anything. She was hyperfocused on the sensation of his hard, shifting body and too mesmerized by his masculine scent. She experienced a nearly overpowering desire to lay her head on his shoulder.

"I don't suppose it would do me any good to ask you why you blew me off in Chicago, would it?" His gruff, quiet voice caused a prickling sensation on her neck.

She flushed and avoided his laserlike stare. "I would think the answer was obvious."

"Nothing is *obvious* when it comes to you and me, Mari. Nothing has ever been easy, either. It was my mother's phone call that did it, wasn't it? That's what made you run? I knew I shouldn't have answered it," he said bitterly. "I only did because I'd been trying for weeks to coordinate communication between my mother and my sister, Deidre, in Germany, and they were supposed to have talked the night before. I had a feeling it might not have gone well for my mother. Their relationship had been strained for years.…"

She met his stare when he faded off. For a moment, she was trapped in his gaze.

"We don't have to dissect the reasons, Marc. Suffice it to say that Chicago was a mistake."

"I don't agree," he stated flatly.

"We'll just have to agree to disagree, then." She noticed the tilt to his jaw—the Kavanaugh pride and stubbornness in full evidence. She sighed and groped for a way to change the volatile topic. "I'd forgotten what a good dancer you are," she murmured.

"I'd forgotten how hard it was to hold you in my arms

and not be able to make love to you later. It's a memory I'd rather put to rest for good, Mari."

Her breath froze on an inhale. His blue eyes blazed hot enough to melt her.

So much for safe topics.

She blinked as if awakening from a trance and took a step away from him. "Don't, Marc."

"Don't what? Make it harder than it already is? Too late," he said softly. His mouth quirked at his double entendre.

Mari was so busy staring at his sexy grin that she didn't resist when he pulled her back into his arms. He didn't miss a beat when the band started playing a slow ballad. The man really could move on the dance floor. As if he needed that extra edge. He was already more attractive to her than he had a right to be.

He gathered her close, so close that Mari became highly conscious of the how thin the barrier of their clothing was, of how little separated them from touching skin to skin.

"Just relax. Didn't anyone ever tell you there's a time for arguing and a time for...dancing?"

The annoyed glance she threw him was more defense than genuine irritation. The truth was, her reaction to Marc worried her. It'd be convenient to say that being around him only evoked all those old feelings, but the reality was, her physical reaction to Marc as a woman was even stronger than it'd been as a girl.

Exponentially so.

Mari held herself rigid as they swayed to the music, but her resistance could only last so long. Her flesh seemed to mold and melt against his of its own accord as if her body recognized its perfect template, even if her brain refused to acknowledge it. A warm sensation settled in her lower belly.

When Marc opened his hand on her lower back and applied a delicious pressure, Mari gave up the fight and rested her cheek between his shoulder and chest. She sighed, inhaling his scent. He smelled delicious—spicy and clean. Her eyes fluttered closed when she felt him lightly nuzzle her hair with his chin. His warm lips brushed against the side of her neck. She shivered. Every patch of skin that his mouth touched seemed to sing with awareness.

When the final note played, her head fell back. She found herself staring into Marc's eyes, which had gone from blazing to smoky. Her breasts were crushed against his chest. The contours of his arousal were abundantly clear to her given how close they pressed.

It was as if a spell had fallen over her. It must have, for her to be having such intimate thoughts—such intimate feelings—in the midst of a crowded, noisy bar.

A crowded, noisy bar in Harbor Town, of all places.

She pulled back from Marc's embrace and touched her fingertips to her cheeks, mortified to feel how hot they were.

"Excuse me," she murmured before she twisted out of his arms.

The water from the ladies' room sink barely cooled her burning cheeks. Her heat had sprung from an inner source that wasn't so easily extinguished. Her eyes closed, she folded a wet paper towel and pressed it to her face, trying to regain her equilibrium.

He could knock her off balance so easily—still and always.

The thought of walking out there and facing Eric and the other patrons mortified her. Marc and she had been practically glued together on the dance floor. At the recollection of Marc nuzzling and kissing her neck—and of her not only allowing it, but loving it—shock washed over her.

She needed to get out of the bar. She needed to get out of Harbor Town altogether, as quickly as possible.

She'd apologize to Eric tomorrow for her abrupt abandonment.

Someone—a woman—called out to her as she fled the noisy establishment. Mari glanced over at the bar and glimpsed Liam and Colleen Kavanaugh watching her. She read excitement and a hint of concern in Colleen's aquamarine eyes. Part of her was glad to see Colleen's willingness to speak with her after all these years, but she was too discombobulated at the moment to renew old friendships. Panic pressed on her chest.

How could she have ever thought it was a good idea to return to Harbor Town? How could she have misled herself into believing Dr. Rothschild when her former therapist had said she had unfinished business in the little town and a bone-deep desire to heal?

She burst out the front door of Jake's Place, gulped the warm, fresh air she'd been oxygen-deprived. It didn't occur to her until she reached the parking lot just what— or who—it was she was escaping. A pair of hands settled on her shoulders and spun her around.

"Marc," she said in a strangled voice. She hadn't realized until that moment she'd been dreading his touch and anticipating it, as well.

"Don't run from me, Mari. Don't run from this."

She swayed closer, to him, inhaling his scent. Nobody smelled like Marc. She wanted to believe that this was something they could solve. Her body wanted to believe him…wanted to trust in Marc, longed to be swept away by a dream.

A girl's dream.

She met his blazing eyes.

"Marc, we can't. Not again," she whispered. She started to move out of their embrace, her fear returning, but he stopped her.

"What is it, Mari? What's your problem with me?" he asked quietly. She saw wariness shadow his face, felt it rising in his tense muscles. "Is it that you think I'm a killer by association? I'm not my father, damn it. I barely finish a beer if I drink at all. I'd throw myself off the top of the Sears Tower before I got behind the wheel of a car drunk. *I* didn't kill your parents."

She blinked in shock at the sudden appearance of his anger. They'd tacitly agreed to stay away from the minefield of this topic in Chicago.

"I never said you did."

"I lost my father in that crash, as well," he said.

Her throat tightened. "I know that. *Surely* you know that."

"I don't know what I'm supposed to think except that you believe I'm guilty by association. I don't know, because you've never really told me, have you? You walked away five weeks ago. You left when we were together and refused to speak to me for fifteen years. One night, we were on the verge of becoming lovers, and the next, we were separated by the news of the crash. Within days, you were gone and thousands of miles separated us, as well."

"Marc, we were kids. I'd lost almost my entire world," she moaned.

"You came back to Harbor Town. You must have had a reason."

"I did have a reason," Mari said. Her gaze deflected off his face. What would he think about The Family Center? Her fantasies about opening it never included having to tell Marc about her plans. What if he thought the project was odd…or worse, self-righteous on Mari's part? He'd probably never understand how much she'd thought of him while making her plans…of the young man she'd loved and lost so many years ago.

She closed her eyes, trying to banish her chaotic thoughts. All she wanted at that moment was to escape this volatile situation with Marc.

"I didn't come back to Harbor Town for you. And I don't want to talk about the past with you, either, Marc."

"Who do you want to talk about it with? Reyes? Is it okay to talk about things with him? Because you're both victims, while I'm the son of the monster who robbed you of your parents?"

"Marc, *don't*. Please."

It pained her more than she could bear to see the raw hurt on his handsome face. A need arose in her to soothe his sadness, to somehow ease his anguish. The knowledge that she was powerless to do so caused the swelling, tight sensation to mount in her chest. She was stunned at how easily that old wound had opened when she saw his expression of disillusionment.

His expression suddenly shifted. He caressed her upper arms in a soothing motion. "Jesus. You're shaking. I'm sorry—"

"What's going on, Mari?"

Mari's eyes widened at the sound of the hard voice behind them. She looked over Marc's right shoulder and saw Eric standing there, looking furious. Marc twisted his chin around.

"Oh, look," Marc muttered with subdued sarcasm. "If it isn't the other victim, here to save Mari from the beast. What are you going to do, Reyes? Start a brawl with me in the parking lot?"

"Marc—" Mari called out warningly, sensing the volatility inherent to the moment.

"No, Kavanaugh. That'd be your M.O., if I recall correctly," Eric replied.

She grabbed hold of Marc's shoulders and tried to get him to face her when he turned toward Eric. "Marc—"

"I'm betting he never bothered to tell you about that. Did he, Mari?" Eric asked. "I know Ryan wanted to keep that story from you—how Kavanaugh clobbered your brother in the parking lot of the courthouse after the judge made his final decision about the lawsuit?" His upper lip curled in contempt, Eric glanced at Marc.

Marc closed his eyes in what appeared to be frustration and mounting anger. After a second, he met her stare. She read regret on his features.

"I thought Ryan would have told you," he said, for her ears only. "I thought maybe that was part of the reason you avoided me all these years."

Something about her expression must have told him the truth—that Ryan never *had* told his little sister about their fight.

"I was twenty-two years old at the time, Mari. It was a long time ago."

Marc and Ryan used to be inseparable, the best of friends. A powerful sadness swept over her.

"Is there a problem?" someone called out sharply.

Eric turned and saw the youngest male Kavanaugh stalking toward them. Mari had heard from Marc that Liam had become a decorated police detective. She could easily believe it was true. He looked like he was about to make a drug bust in a Chicago alley as he stormed toward them.

"Walk away, Reyes," Liam barked, blue eyes blazing. "Why don't you hurry back to that slick house on Buena Vista Drive that my mom's money paid for?"

Eric's mouth dropped open in shock. "You son of a—"

"I wouldn't finish that if I were you," Liam muttered, jaw rigid.

Mari was distantly aware of Jake's front door opening and closing again, but her attention was on the sparks flying between Liam and Eric. Eric's hands were still balled into furious fists.

"What's the matter, Reyes? Worried about bruising those delicate surgeon's hands?" Liam taunted softly. His cocky grin dared Eric to hit him.

Mari groaned when she saw the flash of fury in Eric's dark eyes as he started toward Liam.

"Eric, don't—" Mari called out, but Marc was already moving to intercept them.

"Cut it out, you two," Marc barked. He reached to restrain Eric, his muscles flexing hard beneath his shirt.

But someone else got to Eric first. A hand tapped him on the shoulder. Eric turned, his back to Mari. He remained firmly planted on his feet, but jerked when someone landed a punch on his jaw.

"Leave my brothers alone, Reyes."

Mari gaped when she recognized Colleen Kavanaugh.

"Get her inside right now," Marc growled at Liam, his eyes blazing.

Liam looked like he was chewing nails as he regarded Eric. For a second, Mari worried he'd refuse to obey Marc's taut command, but then he grabbed his sister's arm and murmured to her.

Colleen stumbled on the gravel, her sandaled feet moving reluctantly as Liam led her back to the bar. She twisted around and pinned Eric with a baleful stare. He didn't move, just stood there as if frozen, gazing after the retreating Kavanaughs. Mari heard him curse softly beneath his breath as he stared at Colleen's beautiful, tear-dampened face.

Soon only she, Eric and Marc remained in the parking lot. She couldn't fully identify the expression on Marc's face as his gaze flickered over her, then Eric, then her again. It was as if every imaginable emotion frothed inside him at once in that charged moment. His mouth looked set and hard when he turned and walked toward Jake's Place.

Mari exhaled shakily.

Eric and she regarded each other silently in the dim parking lot lights as the band finished a raucous tune. The final chords faded off in the hot, still summer night. She sensed that Eric knew, as she did, that they'd just narrowly escaped a volatile explosion of emotion.

Nausea rose in her like a striking snake, taking her by surprise. She gagged and bent over, coughing.

"Mari?" Eric's voice sounded shocked and concerned. He touched her back. "Are you okay?"

She swallowed with effort and straightened shakily. "I...I don't know. I just felt sick there for a minute."

"Come on. Let's get you home. This is the last thing you needed to deal with on top of not feeling well."

But as Eric led her to his car, she turned to watch Marc disappear inside Jake's and willfully tamped down the desire to go after him.

Chapter Three

The second Marc joined his mother on the front porch his gaze immediately traveled down Sycamore Avenue to the sandstone, Arts and Crafts-style house down the block. A dark blue sedan sat in the driveway. Mari's car had been notably absent when he'd returned this afternoon from their annual visit to Harbor Town Cemetery.

I didn't come back to Harbor Town for you, he vividly recalled her saying last night. He leaned against the porch railing and crossed his arms below his ribs. What *had* she come back for, then?

He inhaled deeply of the fresh air. It always seemed to take several days into his summer vacation to get the city soot out of his lungs. The sky had turned a pale blue, tinged with lavender, but above the beach at the end of Sycamore Avenue, crimson, pink and gold splashed across the horizon. It would be sunset soon—Harbor

Town's most famous tourist attraction. How many of those sunsets had he watched with Mari in his arms?

He jerked his mind into the present.

"When did you say you were headed back to Chicago?" Brigit Kavanaugh asked. She'd placed her sneakered foot on the pavement, stopping the porch swing's movement.

Marc knew she'd noticed him staring at Mari's house. Not that it was odd for him to look at the Itani vacation home on his rare visits to Harbor Town. His eyes had been trained long ago to stray toward that house. Even his ex-wife, Sandra, used to take note of it, usually with a flippant, sarcastic remark, on the few occasions she'd accompanied him to Harbor Town.

"I was thinking about staying on a couple days past Brendan's party," Marc said, referring to his nephew's tenth birthday celebration.

"Really? Do you think work can spare you that long?"

He shrugged. "The county can undoubtedly do without me."

"Marc," Brigit scoffed with a smile. "You're a state's attorney, for goodness' sake. You have over a thousand employees working under you."

"Most of whom are gone for the holiday. I've never taken off more than day here and there since entering office. I have the vacation time. I might as well use some of it. It's not like I haven't been working from here, anyway."

All of the Kavanaugh children had taken jobs that would somehow prove they were hard-working, sacrificing, *worthy* members of society, Marc mused. His sister Deidre was an Army nurse on her fourth tour of duty. Liam was a twice-decorated detective on the organized crime squad of the Chicago Police Department, and

Colleen was a psychiatric social worker who worked with high-risk teenagers with emotional and substance abuse problems.

Survivors' guilt.

Their father's final actions had left its mark on all of them.

His mother usually wanted her sons to stay on as long as possible for these annual Independence Day visits. She seemed to want Marc long gone at the present time, though. He tried to ignore the flare of irritation he felt at that fact. Brigit loved him. She remembered how much he'd been hurt by Mari's refusal to see him after the crash. Maybe she just didn't want to see him get hurt again.

The porch swing resumed the rhythmic squeaking noise that blended so hypnotically with the sounds of the locusts and the Lake Michigan waves breaking on the nearby beach.

"You'd do best by staying away from her," Brigit said, finally saying the words he knew she'd been thinking since the parades yesterday.

"Maybe you're right. But that doesn't seem to be stifling the urge to do the exact opposite."

Brigit exhaled at his quiet admission. "After all they did to us—"

"Mari never did anything to us. As for what Ryan and his aunt did, it's not that different than what most people would have done in the same situation."

"She ignored you! She took that money—blood money! After all this time, you've forgotten the effect it had on me—on *us*."

"I haven't forgotten," he said, stung. "Maybe it's never occurred to you that Mari and I might have memories, too, Ma, memories outside of Dad and the crash and the deaths—and the *grudge*."

Her face pale and tense, she brought the swing to a halt and stared at him. He hated seeing her pain, but damn it, what he'd said was true. He exhaled heavily, trying to rid himself of his anger. He wasn't mad at his mother, necessarily, but at this whole situation.

He almost heard Brigit building her arguments in her mind. Marc had become a lawyer like his father, but it was his mother who'd taught him the skills for making an airtight case.

"You want Mari because she's the only thing you've wanted and couldn't have."

Marc started. "That's a hell of a thing to say. Do you really believe that?"

"I do," Brigit said quietly. "You're my oldest son, Marc. I carried you in my body, and I watched you grow from an infant to a man. Do you really think I've never noticed that once you set your mind on something, you make it happen, no matter what kind of storm you cause in the process?"

Marc scowled. He couldn't believe he was hearing this from his own mother's mouth. "You make me sound like a spoiled brat. I've worked like hell to get anything I've ever had. And I've failed at plenty of things. What about Sandra?" he demanded.

"I said anything you ever *wanted.* If you'd wanted Sandra more, the two of you would still be married."

Marc gave his mother a hard stare, warning her not to tread on that private territory. He'd heard her out after he and Sandra had decided to split, but that decision was his and his ex-wife's business, not Brigit's. His mother changed gears, just like that.

"Mari never married, I hear," Brigit said levelly.

"No," Marc conceded, not sure where his mother was going with her comment.

"Her brother is the only family since her aunt died a

few years ago. I don't think Ryan would take too kindly to having Mari get involved with you again."

"You really care about what Ryan Itani thinks?"

"No. But if you care about Mari, *you* should. Would you really consider alienating her from her only relative?"

Marc rolled his eyes and stood. "You're assuming Mari would even be interested. I haven't seen any indication of that so far," he muttered bitterly. His mother's comment hit home, even if he tried not to let her see it. He knew he should leave Mari alone. He knew he shouldn't stir up the frothing cauldron of their shared history.

Problem was, he already *had*. He'd touched Mari again. He'd held her naked against him while her shudders of pleasure and release had vibrated into his body and mixed with his own.

It was too late, Marc realized with a grim sense of amazement. Something had happened in those ecstatic moments that couldn't now be ignored.

He noticed movement out of the corner of his eye. He swung around like a hound catching the scent and he saw Mari walking toward her car, her long brown hair bobbing in a ponytail. As she was opening the car door, she paused and looked furtively down the street. Their gazes locked for a few electric seconds before she ducked into the car.

The screen door squeaked open. Combing his longish blonde hair with his fingers in a distracted fashion, Liam sauntered onto the front porch. He looked a little taken aback when Marc charged him.

"Give me the keys to your bike," Marc ordered tersely.

Liam's bewilderment dissipated when he glanced over Marc's shoulder and saw Mari's car backing rapidly out of the driveway. He dug into his short's pocket and handed Marc the keys to his motorcycle.

"Fill it up with gas while you're out, will you? Unless whatever you're doing gets too interesting, that is," Liam said with a mischievous sparkle in his eyes. Marc grabbed the keys and jogged down the porch steps, ignoring his mother's burning glance of disapproval.

Mari had risen early the morning following the Jake's Place fiasco, determined to refocus on her mission. She breakfasted with Eric and Natalie Reyes to discuss more plans for The Family Center. Afterward, she and Eric went to the real estate office to sign a lease, and then to an office furniture and supply store to arrange for items to be delivered to the Silver Dune Bay facility.

She spent the rest of the day making the old house presentable to prospective buyers. Without really knowing why she did it, she paused in her manic scrubbing at 5:17 p.m., walked to the front door and cautiously peeked out a window. A silver sedan passed with three people in it, Marc at the wheel.

She'd somehow known he was near, even though she'd been doing her damnedest to deny his presence in her mind all day. She returned to her cleaning and tried to turn her thoughts in another direction, but failed.

Later that evening, she stood at the front door and gazed onto the tree-lined street. How the hell had she ended up here at this point in her life? Mari wondered. Seeing the crimson sky at the end of the street caused hundreds of other remembered sunsets to blaze to the forefront of her mind. She was hyperaware of the handsome, white house built in the Colonial Revival style up the street.

After the end of a doomed, four-year relationship with James Henry, an investment banker from San Francisco,

Mari had experienced a desire for a fresh start. That inner push had set her plans into motion. She'd wanted to be free of her past once and for all and that meant returning to Harbor Town.

Too bad her grand scheme for a clean slate and healing had turned into a maelstrom of mixed emotions.

By late evening, her stomach had started to growl. She took a shower, pulled her hair into a ponytail and dressed in shorts and a T-shirt. Her heart was skipping rapidly when she exited the house and headed for her car. Something compelled her to look up the street at the Kavanaugh house.

Sure enough, Marc was leaning against the porch railing, his head turned, watching her. For a few seconds, it felt as if she couldn't breathe.

She got in her car and drove to a little diner on the edge of town called The Tap and Grill. After the friendly counter lady had brought her an enormous turkey sandwich to go, she drove aimlessly through the town's quiet, tree-lined streets, finally ending up on scenic Vista Point Drive, overlooking the beach.

A motorcycle roared, breaking the sleepy silence, as she parked at the side of the street. She opened the car door and leaned over to the passenger seat to grab her sandwich. A shadow fell across the steering wheel.

She turned around to see Marc standing between her car and the open door.

"I hope whatever's in that bag is enough for two."

Mari glanced out the back window, noticing the gleaming black and chrome motorcycle parked down the street. She'd peeked out of her windows enough lately to know the vehicle belonged to Liam. Apparently Marc had forsaken a bike years ago for the handsome, conservative sedan she'd seen him driving. Memories of Marc and her brother, Ryan, tearing down the street on their motorcycles, looking like young summertime gods with their deep tans, sunglasses and wind-tousled hair, washed over her.

"Did you follow me?" she asked him warily.

He shrugged, his stare never leaving her face. "I figured you wouldn't answer the door if I knocked at your house. When you finally broke cover, I thought I better take my chance or risk not seeing you for another fifteen years."

She gave him a hard look. He quirked one eyebrow.

"We need to talk, Mari. Please."

Against her will, her gaze lowered to his shadowed jaw and tanned throat. She shivered when she recalled how the stubble had felt brushing against her neck that night in Chicago, grazing ever so lightly against the sensitive skin covering her ribs. The sight of his insouciant male good looks only increased her caution.

Or her reaction to them did.

"So if I let you come with me to Sunset Beach, that's all you'll try to do? Talk?"

He sighed. "I'm not planning on coming on to you on the beach," he replied drily.

She rolled her eyes at him as she aggressively swung her legs out of the car, daring him not to move back and give her the space she required.

His only reaction to her wary acquiescence was a slight grin. They said nothing as they made their way down the private sidewalk that ran between two mansion-sized homes. When they hit the white sand beach, Mari led them over to the manmade breakwater that consisted of stacked lengths of cut, unfinished logs.

She plopped down on the breakwater. Marc sat down next to her. She studied him through the corner of her eye. He wore a pair of cargo shorts and a dark blue shirt that failed to hide the breadth of shoulders or hint at the sleek muscles Mari knew lay just beneath the soft fabric. He managed to make the casual beach-wear look sexy as hell. She could just see him as a tall, lanky, cocky fourteen-year-old sporting a new pair of sunglasses, standing on Sycamore Beach and clutching his skimboard, the sunlight turning his hair into a havoc of incandescent gold waves.

She handed him half of her sandwich wrapped in a napkin.

"I was only kidding about sharing. Eat your supper," he murmured, giving her a sideways smile.

"You know how they make sandwiches at The Tap. It's huge." She insistently pushed the sandwich toward him. Maybe he noticed the irritation in her expression, because his eyebrows rose, and he accepted the food, probably to avoid an argument.

The fiery, orange-red sun looked like it was slowly quenching itself in the shimmering, dark blue water. They ate without speaking. For the first time, it struck her how odd it was that the beach was empty.

"Isn't Sunset Beach public anymore?" she slowly asked Marc as she held up the paper bag so he could deposit his rumpled napkin inside it.

He shook his head. "Mom told me the home owners hereabouts bought it from the town a few years back. It's private now."

Mari stopped chewing and glanced warily at the af-fluent residences nearby.

"Don't worry. They aren't going to call the cops on us. Unless we make an ugly scene or something," Marc said when he saw her uneasiness over trespassing.

She took a swig of the bottled water she'd ordered with the sandwich. She offered the bottle to Marc, and he drank, too. Mari glanced away from the strangely erotic sight of him placing his mouth where hers had just been.

"I don't plan on making a scene," she said briskly, shoving the wrapper and the remainder of her sandwich into the bag. "And you're awfully quiet for someone who insisted we had to talk."

"I just didn't want to ruin the peaceful moment."

She raised her eyebrows. "Implying that whatever you have to say is the opposite of peaceful?"

"If it involves you reacting to it by refusing to see me again... Yeah, there might be some serious waves."

Mari kicked off her flip-flops and stuck her feet in the cool, fine sand. Despite her attempts to calm herself, her voice still cracked when she spoke.

"Marc... You saw what happened last night as well as I did. All that animosity, all that hurt. It'd be irresponsible of us to...you know—"

"I think *I* know, but do *you?*"

"What do you mean?" she asked slowly.

"I wasn't planning this little reunion, Mari. But now that it's happened, I'm not willing to just walk away from it, either. And I'm not talking about sneaking down to your house and having some hot, vacation sex with an old fling." His gaze flickered down over her neck and breasts and he added gruffly, "Although I think we both know that scenario has its appeal. The point is, you mean more than that to me. It was a hell of a thing to see you Chicago and realize that was still true, after all these years. I'm a practical guy. It's kind of hard to run from the truth when it's staring you right in the face."

Mari swallowed thickly in the silence that followed.

"It would never work out," she said after a moment, her voice so quiet it almost couldn't be heard above the sound of the waves breaking gently on the beach.

"I don't think you're so sure about that. I think you want to *act* like you're sure—" her heart surged against her breastbone when he reached up and caressed her jaw with large, gentle fingers "—so it'll be easier to push me away."

Her spine straightened and he let his hand drop to the wood embankment. "I'm not being selfish. I'm trying to be wise," she explained. "I don't want you to be hurt. I don't want my brother to worry. I don't want your mother to be angry. I don't want—"

"What about you? What about what *you* want, Mari?"

She looked out at the dark waters, worrying her lower lip with her front teeth. She was highly aware of him leaning toward her.

"Because here's the thing," Marc muttered near her left ear, causing her neck to prickle in awareness. "I think you were worried about all those things when you left Harbor Town fifteen years ago, when you cut off all ties with me. I think you were thinking about what was *wise* instead of what was *right*."

She glanced at him furtively, but when she saw the expression on his face, her gaze stuck.

"I think you were considering what you thought your parents would have wanted you to do in that situation, Mari."

Anger flared in her breast at his mention of her parents. "I don't have to listen to this."

She started to stand, intent on getting away from him at that moment. He halted her with a firm hand on her shoulder but it was the earnestness in his deep voice that truly restrained her.

"I'm not saying it was wrong. I understand. Your folks were suddenly gone—something you'd never dreamed of as a possibility, even in your worst nightmares—so you did what you thought they would have wanted if they were alive. The rebellious daughter who lied to them and snuck out to see the guy her parents forbade her to see vanished fifteen years ago."

"So what if she did?" Mari challenged. "You're *making* my point, not talking me out of it. I *had* been behaving like a selfish, lying, thankless brat. Sometimes it takes a crisis before you realize how foolish—how hurtful—you've been acting."

"And I'll bet after they died, there were times you would have done anything to take back your rebellion against them," he said quietly. "But there was nothing heartless in what you did, Mari. You were acting like a typical teenager. You never purposely hurt your parents."

"Only because their deaths got in the way of them ever fully realizing what I was doing," she cried out.

"So that's it? You're going to carry around the guilt of a teenage girl inside of you forever? Be a martyr to your parents' cause?" he asked harshly.

This time he didn't succeed in stopping her when she stood. Marc caught up to her several feet away from the surging waves. He placed his hands on her shoulders and turned her around until she faced him.

"I'm not blaming you for feeling guilty, Mari. God knows I haven't been immune to the emotion. I'm not blaming you for staying away for all those years, either. But here's the thing…"

She realized that tears were streaming down her face, even though she hadn't been aware of feeling sadness, only anger and shame and hurt. She stared up into Marc's shadowed face and knew she was experiencing something else in that moment, no matter how tenuous that emotion was.

Hope.

She didn't move, despite her charging heart, when Marc leaned down until their faces were only inches apart. "...you're not an eighteen-year-old girl anymore. You're a woman. Tell me that if you met me for the first time in Chicago that you wouldn't be intrigued by the chemistry between us."

"That's wishful thinking, and you know it," she said in a choked voice. "We *aren't* strangers. We can't escape the past."

"I'm not suggesting we can. But we can deal with it. Or at least we can try."

A shudder went through her at his words. He placed his hand on her back and softly rubbed her, soothing her even though he probably didn't understand her sudden anguish.

We can deal with it.

Was it true? It stunned her to realize that a big part of her doubted they could successfully face their demons.

The realization hurt. Wasn't that why she'd returned to Harbor Town? Because she'd convinced herself there was a chance people could heal, even in the most difficult of circumstances? Did she believe it for other people but not herself?

A moan escaped her throat, and Marc enfolded her in his arms. Hot tears scalded her cheeks, as if they'd been held inside her body for too long and finally boiled over. She pressed her face against his chest. Years of pent-up emotion poured out of her while the waves anointed her bare feet with cold, clean water and Marc held her, helping to ease her anguish.

God, the things she wanted to say to her parents— how sorry she was for not appreciating them more, how much she'd regretted over the years that she hadn't been the daughter they wanted, how much she'd needed their calm, steady presence as a child…how much she loved them.

She'd had similar thoughts thousands of times, but tonight, here on the beach with Marc Kavanaugh's arms surrounding her, Mari knew she'd never fully felt the impact of those regrets.

After several more emotional minutes, Mari slowly became aware of Marc's warm mouth pressing her head as he occasionally murmured to her in a quieting fashion. When he kissed her ear, she shivered in his arms. Her crying slowly ceased as she became more aware of him.

"All I'm asking is that you at least *try*." His rough whisper so near her ear caused her to still in sudden sensual awareness.

"I'm not sure I know how, Marc. It seems like too much, thinking about some of this stuff." She sniffed and turned her face into his shirt. "It's so…"

"What?" he asked quietly.

He cupped the back of her head. She leaned back and looked up at him.

"Big. Intimidating."

"I'm bigger."

She went entirely still when she saw his slow, potent smile cast in moonlight.

"Don't be so cocky," she admonished, even though she couldn't help but smile at his immodesty.

He chuckled and pressed her head back to his chest. "I only meant that I'm stubborn, and more than willing to try." Neither of them spoke for a pregnant moment. "As far as strength goes, I think you're underestimating yourself, Mari. All I'm asking is that you give us a chance. All I'm asking is that you don't run."

He must have sensed her uncertainty, because he spoke coaxingly near her ear.

"Just agree to see me, spend time with me, for the next week or so."

"That's all?" she asked doubtfully.

He drew her against his hard length, making sure she wasn't left in doubt of his desire for her.

"I want you. I always have. I've never made a secret of it...not that I could." She glanced up at him to see his small smile. "But I'll go at your pace. As long as I know you're not running, I'll be happy. Well...at least pacified."

She sighed. She wished she could know it if was right, wished she could be certain.

"Take a risk, Mari."

Her gaze leaped to meet his. Was he a mind reader?

"All right," she whispered. "But I can't guarantee anything. And I want to take things slowly...test out the waters." *See what kind of effect our being seen together has on your family and friends like Eric and Natalie Reyes,* she added privately. She grimaced at her thought, realizing Marc was right to suggest she considered everyone else's feelings before her own.

He pulled her closer. He didn't say anything, but she found herself wondering if he thought the same thing she did. They'd learned fifteen years ago that life was tenuous. People who thought happiness was guaranteed, that security was a certainty, were living in a dream.

But did that mean the dream wasn't worth seeking?

Mari didn't know the answer to that. So she did the best she could. She put her arms around Marc's waist and tried to exist on the knife's edge between doubt and desire. Despite her uncertainties, she became focused on the sensation of Marc's body against hers. She closed her eyes. For a few delicious moments, she was only aware of the soothing sound of the gentle surf and Marc's spicy male scent.

She opened her heavy eyelids when he murmured her name. Much to her amazement, she found herself nuzzling his neck just above his collar, exploring the textures of his skin against her lips. He felt so good. Tasted so good, she added to herself when the tip of her tongue sampled him. He said her name again, more insistently this time. She leaned back and saw the gleam in his eyes as he stared down at her upturned face.

She waited with sharp anticipation while he slowly lowered his head and pressed his lips to hers. It wasn't a chaste kiss, but it was gentle…a promise of passion rather than the thing itself, a sweetness to be savored on her searching lips. She craned up for more of his taste and cried out softly when he lifted his head, depriving her.

"We'd better go," he said, his voice ragged.

"What? Oh…okay," Mari murmured, feeling bereft in the absence of Marc's tender kiss. Hadn't she been the one to tell him not to try anything on the beach, and yet here she was, tempting him into kissing her with all the power she knew he had?

So much for taking things slowly, Mari thought irritably as they went to retrieve the sandwich bag and headed down the lamp-lit sidewalk to the road.

She felt dazed and unsettled about what had just happened out there on that moonlit beach. Had she really just told Marc Kavanaugh she'd see him?

"Uh, I'll see you.… I'd better be…" She fumbled uncertainly after she'd unlocked her car door, highly aware of Marc standing just behind her on the quiet street.

"Yeah. You'll see me."

He sounded so restrained. Wasn't he going to kiss her again? At least touch her?

"Okay, then," she mumbled. "Good night."

He said nothing, increasing her confusion. She slammed her car door and turned the key. Harbor Town seemed as if it'd been cast under a drowsy enchantment, Mari thought as she drove home on the darkened streets. If the kids were out playing on the peaceful summer night, they must be playing hide-and-seek, because she saw no one on her short ride home.

Until she pulled into the driveway and stepped out of her car, that is.

She heard the roar of the motorcycle. Marc pulled up behind her, cut the engine and dismounted the sleek bike. She sensed tension in his shadowed form as he stalked toward her.

"I said I wouldn't accost you on the beach, but I didn't say a word about your front yard."

He took her into his arms and covered her mouth with his.

This kiss was everything his former one was not: hot, consuming. He spanned her upper back with his hands in a blatant gesture of ownership, her breasts pressing tightly against his ribs.

Mari moaned as he explored her mouth thoroughly, and she submitted to his bold claim. She wrapped her arms around his waist and held on while lust surged in her blood, enlivening her flesh. It never occurred to her to question the sudden inferno of her desire. Logic and the result of Marc's kisses were mutually exclusive events.

She panted softly when he lifted his head only to lower it again and press his mouth to her neck. She couldn't think straight with him nibbling and kissing, his teeth occasionally gently scraping her skin, causing her nipples to tighten in excitement. His hands moved over her, coaxing her to enter a sensual fog. She leaned her head back, granting him more access. Her eyelids parted into slits, and she found herself staring at the dim streetlight.

A quick, flashing picture arose in her imagination—Brigit Kavanaugh standing on her front porch, staring down Sycamore Street as her son publicly ravished Mari Itani in her driveway.

"Marc," she whispered hoarsely. "People will see."

For a moment, she thought he hadn't heard her as he continued to ravenously explore her neck with his mouth, but then he abruptly stopped. He grabbed her hand and pulled her toward a lush maple tree. Mari jogged after him. The tree's thick canopy of leaves provided a cover the streetlight couldn't penetrate.

He positioned her with her back against the tree trunk and immediately swooped down to kiss her again. Their private, adult game of hide-and-seek on this hot, Harbor Town night only increased her ardor, She didn't respond passively but caught his tongue and created suction, loving his raspy groan of arousal in response.

Heat flooded her lower belly and sex. She sighed in sublime satisfaction at his hard pressure against her tingling flesh. She knew firsthand just how much Marc Kavanaugh wanted her in that moment, and it was delicious, heady knowledge.

His stroking hand encircled her neck and then found a breast. He fondled the sensitive flesh with a knowing touch, making her kiss even more hungry…more desperate. A moment later, he lifted his head. The night surrounded them like enfolding velvet as Marc lifted her T-shirt up over her breasts.

Mari moaned when she felt pleasure pinch at her nipple and simultaneously between her thighs. Marc's long fingers moved, scooping the flesh over the top of her bra, pushing down the cup. His fingertips whispered across the now-naked, puckering nipple, and Mari bit her lower lip to keep from crying out.

"Such beautiful breasts," he whispered before he molded her flesh into his warm palm and continued to pluck the crest.

Mari whimpered as her desire swelled into full bloom. And when his warm mouth enfolded her nipple, she couldn't prevent herself from crying out. His tongue was the gentlest tease one moment and a demanding lash the next. She shifted her hips restlessly. Marc must have instinctively understood how she ached, because he palmed the juncture between her thighs.

Mari's eyes sprang wide as pleasure jolted through her flesh. This was crazy. They were in her front yard, for goodness' sake. Things had moved from an impassioned kiss to heavy petting so quickly that she'd lost all good sense.

And she'd said she wanted to take things slow. How could Marc take her body from room temperature to boiling so fast?

When Marc deftly began to unfasten her shorts, she protested, but very weakly. "Marc, we really shouldn't."

She gasped at the sensation of his long fingers slipping beneath the silk of her panties. When she felt him find the evidence of her arousal, he groaned harshly. Mari leaned her head against the tree trunk, gasping and whimpering while Marc stoked her body into a raging fire. When she cried out anxiously, he muttered next to her lips.

"Let go, Mari. I'm here. I've got you."

Marc.

Always tempting her senses, teasing her into feeling her courage. She found herself responding as she always had to his challenges. He put his left arm around her, holding her against his body when she shattered.

The lulling sound of the locusts penetrated her consciousness. She blinked her eyes open slowly as convulsions of pleasure still shimmered through her flesh.

"See, Mari? Your body trusts me. You just have to let your mind trust me, as well." He kissed her, quick, fierce…hungry.

"Let's go inside," he said.

Mari heard his gruff voice through a thick haze of combined arousal and satiation. She opened her mouth, an agreement on her tongue, when someone called out from the sidewalk.

"Marc?"

Mari's breath froze on an inhale.

"Liam?"

Marc's response made her jump. She frantically pushed away from him and started righting her mussed clothing.

"Uh, sorry to bother you," Liam called. "I saw the bike."

She put her hands on Marc's shoulders and shoved. "Go on. Talk to him," she whispered. Even in the midst of her mortification and disbelief at her wantonness, Mari missed his hard heat.

"I got a call from my captain," she heard Liam say. "I need to get back to Chicago tonight, but I should make it back for Brendan's birthday party. Mom said you were staying. Can I take your car? You can keep the bike and we'll switch when I get back."

Mari felt like a fool standing in the dark shadows of the tree when Liam surely knew she was there. She smoothed her hair, but there was nothing she could do about the heat and color in her cheeks—the telltale signs of her impulsivity when it came to Marc. She held her chin up as she joined the two men at the edge of the yard.

"Well, as I live and breathe, if it isn't Mari Itani," Liam said, deadpan.

She met Liam's amused glance and broke into a grin. She couldn't help it. Liam had always made her laugh.

He held out his arms invitingly. "Give me a hug, girl. We never got around to saying hello last night."

She went willingly, gasping when Liam squeezed her so tight her breath whooshed out of her lungs. Marc tapped his brother's elbow after several seconds.

"Haven't you got some emergency in Chicago?" Marc prompted.

"Oh, right," Liam agreed. He grinned devilishly as he released Mari. "I guess I should let you two get back to whatever emergency you were attending to behind that tree."

Mari glanced at Marc furtively. "Don't hurry away on my part, Liam. I was just about to go inside."

"Mari," Marc growled a quiet warning, which she ignored.

"Good night, both of you. Liam…it was wonderful to see you," Mari said before she hurried toward the house.

"Nice timing," she heard Marc say with dark sarcasm.

She flew up the front porch steps to the sound of Liam's low, male laughter.

Chapter Four

The beachgoers would love the new day, Mari decided. She peered through the screen door the next morning. Bright sunshine had turned Sycamore Avenue into a picture of small-town Americana, complete with white-washed fences and robins twittering in the lush, mature oaks and maples.

She glanced toward the top of the street, her gaze lingering on the Kavanaugh house. It stunned her, how nervous she was about seeing Marc again. How excited.

He was just a man, after all.

But she was lying to herself, and she knew it. She'd never reacted to anyone as she had to Marc. She'd done her share of dating over the years and almost married James. Several of those men, most notably James, had accused her of being obsessed with her career—aloof and distant.

Some quirk of nature had made her anything but aloof with Marc.

She turned her attention back to the house, determined to tackle the dusting before the day got away from her. Surely she had more practical things to consider at the moment besides reigniting an old flame.

She retrieved some rags and lemon-scented polishing oil and buried herself in some honest, physical labor.

A wave of nausea forced her down the ladder several hours later. She supposed she should eat something. She pushed a few tendrils that had come unbound off her perspiration-damp face. Applying some elbow grease to what seemed like miles of mahogany built-ins, wainscoting and trim really worked up a sweat. She was in the kitchen eating some crackers to calm her stomach when she heard footsteps on the front porch.

She froze. It was him; she just knew it. With a mixture of trepidation and anticipation, she went to the screen door.

It was Marc, all right. He waited at the door, his arms crossed beneath his chest, his knees slightly bent. He leaned back on his heels in a relaxed, thoroughly male pose. Their gazes immediately met through the screen door. She saw his eyes flicker briefly down before he met her stare again. At that brief visual caress, her nipples prickled in awareness against the fabric of her bra and form-fitting T-shirt.

"Is that her?" someone asked in a hushed voice.

Marc's jaw tilted sideways even though he continued to meet Mari's gaze. "That's her." Marc's voice lowered in a mock conspiratorial whisper to the young boy who stood next to him.

Marc wasn't alone on her front porch. She hadn't initially noticed, thanks to Marc's powerful presence. No sooner had she seen the tall boy when another child— this one sporting a long, white-blond ponytail—peeked around Marc's thigh.

"Hello," the little girl said.

"Hi," Mari replied, charmed by the child's huge, blue eyes and sober expression.

She opened the screen door. Her gaze flickered up to Marc, who was warmly watching her. Leave it to him to bring the two children—his niece and nephew?—to lighten the tension of their meeting.

Marc touched the top of the little girl's head. "You can come out of hiding, Jenny. Mari won't bite. I don't think so, anyway."

She rolled her eyes at Marc before she smiled and beckoned her visitors into the house.

"You two wouldn't be Colleen's kids, would you?" Mari asked over her shoulder as she led them down the hallway to the kitchen. She'd heard that, unlike the other Kavanaughs, Colleen had married and had children.

"Yes, Colleen Sinclair is our mom," the boy said. His adult tone made Mari's smile widen.

"Marianna Itani, meet my niece and nephew, Jenny and Brendan," Marc said as they entered the sunny kitchen.

"You said her name was Mari, not Marianna," Jenny said to her uncle under her breath, as if she was politely trying to correct his error.

"Mari is short for Marianna like Jenny is for Jennifer," Marc explained.

"Oh," Jenny uttered while she studied Mari with interest. "You look like a princess."

"Jenny," Brendan groaned, clearly embarrassed by his little sister's forthrightness.

Mari smiled at the girl. "Thank you. You look very much like your mother did when she was close to your age. And it's a pleasure to meet both of you. Would you like something to drink? Some lemonade?" she added when both children nodded.

Mari poured lemonade and searched through her meager groceries for a snack that might tempt the children. She found a small bag of gourmet, chocolate chip cookies and placed several on a plate. Marc watched her while the kids looked around the large kitchen with interest.

"Brendan told me this house was haunted," Jenny said as Mari handed her a glass of lemonade and set the cookies on the oak table.

"I did not," Brendan said, blushing. He was blond, like his sister, although his hair was a shade or two darker. He obviously had already spent a lot of time at one of Harbor Town's white sand beaches, given his even, glowing tan. Despite Brendan's dark eyes, Mari couldn't help but be reminded of Marc at a similar age.

"You *did*. Every time we play outside after dark at Grandma's, you say it," Jenny replied before she took a sip of her lemonade and daintily picked up a cookie.

Mari glanced at Marc, and they shared a secret smile. As a child, Colleen had been both a lady and a hellraiser. It seemed her daughter shared a similar bent.

"Do you mind if we look around?" Brendan asked Mari.

"Feel free, although there isn't much to see," Mari said. "Least of all any ghosts, I'm afraid."

Brendan looked slightly disappointed at this.

"Leave your lemonade on the counter," Marc directed before the children scurried out of the kitchen.

Mari glanced at Marc, laughter in her eyes. "They're beautiful."

"Yeah," Marc agreed. "They're great kids. It's Brendan's birthday the day after tomorrow. He'll be ten, but I swear, sometimes it feels like he's about to turn thirteen."

"Wants to be fully independent already, huh?"

She heard one of the children speak in the distance. It struck her suddenly that she was alone here in the kitchen with Marc.

"Yeah. Colleen has her hands full with Brendan." Marc's low murmur made Mari think he might have become just as aware of her in that moment as she had him. "He keeps needling to let him go to the beach with his friends—no supervision."

"We used to go on our own at Brendan's age," Mari mused.

"Yeah, but we grew up in a different world. Our parents were lucky to see us for meals, and they wouldn't have seen us then, either, if we weren't starving. We lived on the beach during the summer."

They shared a smile at their memories. She recalled the golden afternoons, taking a break from her adventures with the Kavanaugh children and to return to Sycamore Avenue for dinner, her mother humming while she cooked, her father on the back terrace reading the newspaper from cover to cover or ineffectively trying to make his creeping hydrangeas bloom. Mari and Ryan would bolt their meals and dash outside again to play freeze tag or Red Rover with the Kavanaughs until one of their parents' voices rang out in the night, ending their summertime bliss until the next morning when it would resume again with the fresh promise of a new day.

"Looks like you've been working hard," Marc said, nodding at the wood cleaner and mounds of dust cloths on the counter.

"I'm trying to get the house in shape to be sold."

"Seems sad, thinking about someone else living here. I have a lot of memories about this old house."

"Yeah," she whispered, studying his strong profile as he glanced around the room.

A half hour later, the children sat cross-legged on the front porch while they played *Operation*. The batteries in the toy had long since petered out, but Brendan and Jenny didn't seem to mind. Each just watched with a tight focus as the other removed the little plastic bones from the tiny holes in the patient and called foul when they believed the surgical instrument had touched the edges of the wound.

Much to Mari's amazement, Brendan had discovered a closet in the basement filled with old board games, mementos and photos and even a few of Mari's and Ryan's yearbooks. She hadn't been the one to clear out the Dearborn family home years ago; Ryan had seen to that. Most of the furniture had been sold at an auction after their parents' deaths, although she and Ryan had kept some pieces from both homes. Ryan must have brought some of their belongings from Dearborn to Harbor Town years back. It made her a little melancholy to think of her brother carefully storing away those remnants of their childhood.

"Who did Colleen marry?" Mari asked Marc, who sat next to her on the porch swing.

"Darin Sinclair."

Noticing his hushed tone, Mari glanced over at him.

"Colleen met him while they were both at Michigan State. Darin was an Army ranger. He was killed in Afghanistan almost two years ago."

Mari's gaze zoomed over to Brendan and Jenny, their blond heads bent over the board game, speaking to each other in low tones. Suddenly Colleen's children's adult manners made perfect sense. They'd lost their father so young....

Maybe Marc noticed her shocked expression, because he grabbed one of her hands in both of his. He rubbed her wrist with a warm, slightly calloused palm. She shivered.

"I'm sorry I mentioned it," he said. "I understand Ryan is stationed in Afghanistan. He's in the Air Force, isn't he?"

Mari blinked. "Yes. Ryan's a Captain…a pilot. He's stationed in Kabul. He'll be coming home to San Francisco in two weeks. I'm counting the days." She put her other hand on top of his, accepting the comfort he offered her without conscious thought. Tears smarting in her eye, she glanced up at him. "I wasn't thinking about Ryan just now, though. I was thinking… It seems so *unfair,* after everything Colleen went through as a kid, to have to endure more as an adult."

His expression turned grim. The next thing she knew, his arm was around her, and her head was on his shoulder. The porch swing squeaked as they swayed. Mari watched Brendan and Jenny play while Marc stroked her upper arm, and she breathed in his scent.

"Do you know what I think, Mari?" he asked after a moment. "I think you've had enough of cleaning house and being sad. I think you and I need to go to the beach."

She lifted her head and looked at him. He wore a small smile, and his expression carried just the hint of a playful dare.

"I shouldn't," she whispered. "I have so much to do."

"Like what?"

Mari hesitated. It would have been a good moment to broach the topic of The Family Center. His mood was so light, though, so warm. She found herself wanting to avoid the weighty subject.

Or perhaps she was just a coward, and was avoiding having him misunderstand her intentions…judge her.

She waved lamely toward the house. "I have cleaning to do."

"There are better things to do on a gorgeous day like today than dust, Mari."

She gave a bark of laughter. Confronted with Marc's wry challenge, she couldn't seem to help it. It was so strange to feel this swelling surge of life, like sap rising in an old tree. She'd grown so used to being careful to maintain her control, of walling off the impulsive side of her nature that she only knew existed because of the man who sat next to her.

"I don't have a swimsuit," she said, her gaze locked on his well-shaped mouth.

"Colleen and Deidre left a dozen suits over the years. I saw them behind the towels in the linen closet. Come on," he said. "There are still some good times to be had in Harbor Town. The only thing that's required is that you let them happen."

She had a hundred other things to do besides idle away the day on the beach with Marc. Still, part of her clung to the promise in his blue eyes.

"The real estate agent is going to be here any minute," she stalled.

"Perfect. I have some work to finish up before we go. The meeting with the agent isn't going to take all day, is it?"

"No, but…" She paused when he gave her a pointed glance.

"You always get your way, don't you," she said softly.

Her heart squeezed in her chest at the sight of his potent grin.

"That remains to be seen, but I'm the optimistic type. How about if I pick you up at two?"

* * *

Later that afternoon, Marc waited on Mari's front porch while she changed into the swimsuit he'd brought. He'd kept his expression impassive when she'd given him a *you've got to be kidding me* look when he'd handed her the bikini.

"There's more air than material to this thing," she'd accused as she'd held up the skimpy bathing suit.

"What?" he'd asked innocently. "You used to wear bikinis all the time."

"I'm not a teenager anymore. Honestly," she'd scolded.

He'd glanced over her. "You've got even more of a reason to wear a bikini now than you did when you were seventeen, Mari."

The roll of her eyes had told him she thought he was full of it, but Marc had only been telling the absolute truth. The vision of Mari naked in the Palmer House Hotel's room would undoubtedly be burned into his memory until the day he died. Her beauty had matured into the type that could make a man a little nuts, if he let it.

He glanced up when the screen door opened and Mari walked out onto the porch. Her brown hair was up on her head, but a few wisps of it fell around her flushed cheeks. She wore a red tank top and jean shorts that showed off her long, shapely legs. He let his gaze trail over the sight of bare shoulders that reminded him of smooth honey. His body responded to the sight of her like a cord jerked tight.

Still. After all these years.

"All set?" he asked gruffly as he stood.

She nodded and glanced away. He'd started to get used to Mari's hesitancy around him—her nervousness. When he saw the color in her cheeks deepen, he wondered if it'd truly been anxiety she'd been experiencing, though.

He'd already picked up a lunch for them from The Tap and Grill. After he'd stowed it and the canvas bag she carried in the storage receptacles on Liam's bike, he noticed Mari's expression.

"What?" he asked.

"I'd forgotten we would be—" she waved vaguely at the motorcycle "—you know...using Liam's bike."

He knew what she was thinking, and he thought it was best not to comment. She, too, recalled driving around Harbor Country years ago, the cycle vibrating with power beneath them, Mari pressed so tightly against his hips and back that not even a granule of the white, sugary sand from one of the beaches could have made its way between them.

He just grinned and handed her a helmet. Her wariness faded when she took in his expression. He was relieved to see her lips curve in amusement. He'd expected her to insist on taking her rental car instead of the bike. She was in the process of fastening the helmet when she paused. Marc glanced up the street where she was staring. He saw his mother standing at the top of the steps of her house. She was watching them.

"Let's go," he said quietly, noticing how Mari's smile had faded at the sight of Brigit. "That sun is broiling me. I need a swim."

He straddled the leather seat. The engine roared to life. He waited while Mari climbed on. When he felt the pressure of her thighs surrounding his and her arms around his waist, he took off down the driveway, the feeling of Mari's supple body pressing against him, making him forget his mother's condemning glare.

"Where are we going?" he heard Mari shout behind

him after they'd ridden down Route 6 for ten minutes or so.

"Tranquil Lagoon. Have you ever been?" he asked over his shoulder.

"No, it doesn't sound familiar."

"Colleen introduced me to it a couple of years back. Most of the locals don't even know it exists." .

After following a serpentine road that branched from the rural highway to a drive that consisted of crumbling concrete and burrowing weeds, Marc stopped the motorcycle at the top of a bluff and shut off the engine.

"We'll have to walk the rest of the way," he said.

He grabbed the two bags and headed down a grassy trail that sloped at a steep angle. Mari slid in her tennis shoes, fell into him and apologized. He turned and took her hand while she righted herself.

His body buzzed with a sexual tension that was getting increasingly difficult to ignore. He'd told Mari he'd go slowly with her, and he'd do his best to stand by his word. He was a man, not a saint, though. And Mari tempted him like he couldn't recall ever being tempted.

He kept her hand in his once she'd steadied herself. They picked their way down the steep, overgrown path. Several large locust, elm and oak trees blocked the view of the lagoon when they reached the bottom of the surrounding dunes. When they broke away from the cover of the trees, he heard Mari gasp in pleasure.

"Oh, it's lovely," she murmured as she stared out onto the horseshoe-shaped body of water. Massive dunes surrounded the inlet on three sides. Its choppy waters a brilliant blue that reflected the cloudless summer sky, Lake Michigan sparkled outside the narrow mouth of the lagoon. The lagoon absorbed both the hue of the sky and the surrounding foliage, making it a deep teal. The placid waters made a perfect mirror for the lush green trees.

Marc led Mari over to a spit of sand at the edge of the water. No one else was in sight. He set down their bags in the shadow of a large white boulder and whipped off his shirt. Mari did a double take at his rapid disrobing.

"What? I'm burning up," he said. Not just from the hot sun, either, he thought wryly as he considered the last quarter of an hour spent with Mari pressed against him, the hum of the motorcycle only increasing his sensual awareness of the woman behind him. He kicked off his shoes and waved at her clothing. "Come on. Don't tell me you don't want to take a dip."

"I do." She seemed a little dazed.

The way she was staring at his chest made him forsake courtesy. He headed toward the lagoon. He needed a slap of cold water against his skin. It wasn't going to do him any good to stand there and watch Mari strip down to that little bikini he'd brought her, as much as he wanted to do just that.

He resurfaced from a short swim a minute later and turned toward the shore. He saw Mari standing waist deep in the water and swam toward her. She was smiling at him when he surfaced five feet away.

"Feels good, huh?" he asked.

He was captivated by her eyes as she nodded. She had the most beautiful eyes he'd ever seen—a rare color, like brown infused with amber.

"It feels wonderful. The water is a little warmer than the lake itself this time of year," she said and moved her hands as though caressing the surface of the lagoon.

Marc's gaze traveled up the path of an elegant arm and lingered on a smooth shoulder. The need to touch her swelled in him, but he refrained.

With effort.

"I see the suit fits all right," he said as he glanced at her breasts, barely restrained behind two scraps of gold cloth.

"Get that grin off your face, Kavanaugh," Mari said, rolling her eyes.

"Am I grinning?" Marc laughed, ruining his innocent look.

"You know you are."

He continued to chuckle as she plunged into the water, covering herself from his gaze. She surfaced several feet away from him, standing in water that covered her from the chest down. She wiped the water out of her face and gave him a censorious look.

"It's one of Deidre's swimsuits," she said reprovingly. "You know how small she is. One of Colleen's would fit me much better. Not that I'm telling you anything you don't know," she said, giving him a disgusted look.

"Do you think I notice stuff like that? They're my sisters, for Christ's sake."

"You never noticed that Deidre is petite and delicate?"

He snorted. "I don't know what you remember about Deidre, but my sister is anything but delicate. She's been known to run into the line of fire and hoist a wounded soldier over her shoulder before carrying him to safety."

"She did that?" Mari asked, her eyes going wide.

Marc nodded, not particularly fond of this latest example of his sister's reckless bravery. "She won the Army Medal of Honor for it. Thank God, she's been transferred to Germany, far from active battle."

"You must worry about her a lot," Mari said as she took a step closer.

"Like you do about Ryan," he murmured.

A hush fell over them. A robin twittered in the distance.

"I'm sorry about the way you found out about Ryan and me fighting after the trial all those years ago," he said.

She glanced up at him, her sad, sober gaze tearing at him a little.

"You weren't there, Mari. To say emotions were running high during the court proceedings is a huge understatement."

"You and Ryan used to be so close," she whispered. "Sometimes…" She stared at the narrow opening to the blue lake and made a hissing sound of frustration.

"What?"

She shook her head. "I just wish the crash had never happened."

"You're still angry about it."

Her gaze shot to meet his. "I didn't say that!"

"It wouldn't surprise me if you were. Who wouldn't be angry about having their parents unexpectedly stolen from them one stormy summer night?"

He saw her throat convulse as she swallowed. He realized he was holding his breath when she took another step toward him in the cool water.

"My parents weren't the only thing I lost," she whispered.

Desire sliced through him as he looked down at her face. He held himself on a tight leash, but he didn't want Mari to know that. Not at that moment, he didn't.

"If you're referring to me, I'm standing right here," he replied.

She started, blinked and looked away. "I *was* referring to you. But I was referring to more than that. I was thinking of my childhood. My security. My belief that everything would always be the same.… That even when things got bad, I'd wake up the next day, and everything would be fresh and new. I lost all of that, that summer," she said softly.

"We all did."

"I know," she said quickly. "I know it. I meant to tell you that the other night in the parking lot, but things got out of hand so fast. I never blamed you, Marc. Never. How could I?"

He shrugged. "Other people managed to. It's human nature. When the perpetrator of the crime dies along with the victims, people look to the family. Blame has to be cast somewhere."

"But that's ridiculous!"

"I'm not saying it isn't. But people need to do something with their anger, with their helplessness." He shrugged. "I see it all the time in my work. Victims need to find a target for their angst. My mother has lived with that refrain for fifteen years. In the beginning, she got nasty phone calls, hate mail, pranks were pulled. People in town ostracized her. Some of them still do. It hasn't been an easy road for her. People say she should have been harder on my dad about his drinking. Maybe one of us kids should have stopped him somehow. Maybe *I* should have. I was old enough. That was what my opponent for the State's Attorney position thought…and made a point of mentioning about a dozen times during the campaign," he added wryly under his breath.

"You're kidding."

He shrugged and glanced away. In all honesty, he'd repeatedly wondered if he might have done something to prevent the crash.

"You were twenty-one years old," she whispered. "Please tell me you don't actually believe any of those allegations."

"No. I don't," he said after a moment. "My dad

was responsible for his actions. Does that mean those criticisms didn't eat at me at times? Of course not. It's natural to wonder how you could have done things differently."

"How could you have known what your father was going to do on that night? You had your own life. You hardly were thinking about *Derry* any more than I was thinking of *my* parents at the time."

She'd spoken in a pressured rush. Marc recognized the moment she realized what she'd just said. Color rushed into her cheeks.

Of course neither of them had thought of their parents that night. They'd been in bed together, their love on the brink of consummation.

Marc shoved aside the emotion-packed memory with effort.

"Deidre holds my mother responsible for a lot of what happened with the crash. She thinks my mother was in denial about my father's drinking problem. That's why she doesn't return to Harbor Town in the summer like the rest of us. Actually, Deidre refuses to come to Harbor Town, period."

Marc sighed when he saw Mari's horrified expression. He'd brought her here for a casual outing, a chance for them to reconnect over something besides their volatile past.

"Let's not worry about it, okay? Not now," he murmured.

He gave in to his need and placed his hands on her damp shoulders. She went still beneath his touch. He slipped a finger beneath the cloth of the swimsuit where it tied around her neck.

"I just thought the color would look good on you, that's all." He noticed her confused expression. "That was the reason I picked this suit. The main reason, anyway," he said as he watched himself idly stroke her. He met her stare. "Gold—like your eyes and your skin."

"Marc."

Her breath fell across his lowering mouth. He kissed her softly, and she responded to his coaxing caresses, feeding his desire with a distilled sweetness he associated exclusively with Mari. His muscles tensed when he felt her fingertips touch his chest, her movements striking him as curious but uncertain, featherlight and quick, like ten drops of water scurrying over his skin. It hurt a little to feel his body respond so wholeheartedly to her taste and feel and to have to restrain himself, holding back what seemed so natural and right. When they'd been young, it'd been a serious trial.

As an adult man, it was nothing less than torture.

Her eyes seemed to smolder beneath her heavy eyelids when he finally lifted his head to study her. The need to press her soft, lithe body against his length in the calm water nearly choked him, it felt so powerful. He placed his thumb, a placeholder for his mouth, on her lower lip and rubbed, a reminder to Mari that while he'd do his best, there was only so much a man could do to control human nature.

"I'll race you to the mouth of the lagoon."

"What?" she asked, looking dazed and beautiful.

"I'm trying to control myself, Mari, but it's hard."

Her eyes widened at his abrupt, gruff statement. She blinked, as though coming out of a trance.

"All right, let's swim then," she said breathlessly.

Thankful for the rush of coolness across his overheated body, he submerged himself in the water.

Chapter Five

They swam, and they ate the sandwiches Marc had brought and they swam again. They talked almost non-stop, as though they were trying to make up for fifteen years of separation in one afternoon. Mari hesitantly asked him about his divorce, but she soon discovered there was no reason for discomfort on that front. Marc spoke without rancor about his ex-wife. He explained how they'd grown apart and how they'd wanted different things.

"I suppose that can happen to any couple," Mari murmured, thinking of herself and James as she idly dried herself with a towel. "People grow. They change. There's no guarantee they'll change in the same way."

"Maybe," Marc replied levelly. "But if you care enough about the person to begin with, there's more of a cushion to weather the changes."

He sprawled on the blanket to soak up the sun's rays. He went on to tell Mari that Sandra had disapproved wholeheartedly of him running for Cook County State's Attorney, and how his choice had been the nail in the coffin of their marriage.

"She insisted I only wanted experience at the State's Attorney's Office as a springboard for a cushy job at a law firm. When I said I planned to run for the job, she couldn't believe it."

Mari didn't reply for several seconds as she studied his strong profile. "I've heard that you head up the second largest criminal justice system in the entire country. It's an extraordinary feat, Marc. I…I was really proud of you when I heard you'd won the election."

He lifted his head off the blanket. "You were?"

She rolled her eyes, both flattered and discombobulated by the fact that he seemed genuinely pleased by her compliment. "Of *course*. Do you—" she glanced away from his piercing eyes "—regret it?"

"Becoming a state's attorney?"

"No. You and Sandra splitting."

He exhaled and lay back, staring up at the blue sky and fluffy clouds. "No. It was the right thing to do. If anything, I regret entering into the marriage so impulsively. I was too young. Maybe I was grasping for something to hold on to."

He glanced over and noticed her small smile.

"What?" he asked.

Mari shook her head and looked away from the enticing vision of him lying there wearing nothing but board shorts and water droplets.

"I was just thinking you must be one of the most eligible bachelors in the state."

He rolled his eyes. "If anyone thinks that, they're either crazy or have never experienced the fallout of divorce. I hardly consider myself to be in the marriage market. Avoiding it like the plague, more like. What about you? Do you have any regrets, Mari?"

"With my career? No. I've never once regretted my work. You must remember how much I loved playing, even when I was a girl. My choice of career was an easy one. I've felt nothing but blessed since the day someone actually paid me to do what I love."

"You're fortunate."

"I am. Maybe too much so."

His brows went up.

She laughed self-consciously. "I've had a boyfriend or two tell me that I'm *too* serious about my career."

"Ah. We have that in common, then. Fortunate in our choice of career, unlucky at love. It's funny, though.... I'd always pictured Mari Itani to be the type to master both her career and romance like a pro." His mouth quirked with humor, but his eyes were warm as they studied her. "Figured you'd be married with at least five kids by now and be busy training them for the family orchestra."

Mari whipped her towel at him in playful reprimand. Hearing Marc tease her had caused embarrassment and pleasure to surge through her in equal measure. There was little doubt she'd once expected to settle down and start a family with him.

Funny, how the dreams of a girl still had the power to move her.

Soon, the sun's warm rays lulled Mari as she lay on the blanket they'd spread on the beach. Admiring the gleam and flex of his strong back muscles, she watched through heavy eyelids as Marc again wandered into the lagoon to cool off and swim.

When she awoke, her right cheek was pressed against her extended arm. She glanced around sleepily, not moving her head, wondering why she felt so content when she wasn't immediately certain where she was. She saw the blue-green water of the lagoon wink in the periphery of her vision and recalled the day in a flash. Everything was quiet.

Where was Marc?

She abruptly turned onto her back and bumped into the answer to her question. He was right there—his arm bent at the elbow, his head in his hand, his long body curved around her. Only an inch or two separated them. She laughed in startled amazement when she saw his blue eyes studying her.

"What are you doing?" she asked.

"What does it look like I'm doing?" he countered in a low, husky voice that only added to her sense of delicious lassitude.

"It looks like you were watching me sleep." His gaze flickered over her neck and breasts, and made her skin tingle.

He smiled. She stared up at him, mesmerized by the longing in his blue eyes. "I was thinking about all the nights I missed watching you while you slept," he replied in a hushed tone.

A strained silence ensued.

"Did you think about me? When you left for San Francisco?" he asked.

"How can you ask me that?" Her eyes burned when she blinked. "It was hell, that first year after the crash. My aunt was worried sick about me, I lost so much weight and I couldn't sleep through the night. I'd wake up in a panic."

"Were you having nightmares?"

She shook her head. "I'd dream I was back in Michigan and that everything was perfect. I'd dream my parents were still alive. I'd dream of being with you again."

She reached up and caressed his jaw. "Waking up was the nightmare."

His nostrils flared slightly at her words. His eyes looked fierce. He leaned down and pressed his mouth to hers.

She sighed in surrender. It was just the two of them. They weren't hurting anyone by acknowledging their unique bond. The past receded. Surely there was nothing stronger than this moment, than this feeling?

He lifted his head too soon for Mari.

"Marc?" she whispered, disappointed at his withdrawal.

His mouth slanted in irritation. He glanced up at the thick foliage behind them.

"What—?" she asked, startled when he abruptly sat up. Mari heard voices behind them. She sat up, as well, twisting to look behind her.

Three teenagers—two girls and a boy—reached the bottom of the path and walked onto the white sand. They hesitated when they saw they weren't alone, but then the boy said something Mari couldn't catch, and they headed down the spit of sand, granting Mari and Marc space, if not privacy.

Marc glanced back at her, the heat in his eyes still very much present, and gave her a wry smile. She laughed softly. They were a little old to get caught fooling around on the beach. She tried to ignore the sharp stab of regret she experienced and reached for her tank top.

They dressed and packed up their belongings, speaking sparingly to each other as they trudged back up the steep path. She noticed how far the sun had dipped in the western sky as Marc got on the motorcycle.

"How long did I sleep?" she asked as she climbed up behind him.

"Over an hour."

"Really?" she asked, flustered. It was out of character for her to nap for so long, if at all. Had Marc watched her that whole time? "I'm sorry. I've been a little tired ever since the trip," she murmured as he shifted the cycle to an upright position.

"Don't be. I didn't mind." The bike roared to life.

Mari had thought the spell that had settled on them in the lagoon had been broken by the arrival of the teenagers, but she'd been wrong. She held on tight to Marc's waist and pressed her chest to his back, her cheek to his shoulder and watched the trees and picturesque farms pass by as he drove on country roads for miles. When Marc turned the bike down a long, narrow drive, she noticed a handmade sign featuring a peach and a fluffy pie: McKinley Farm and Orchard—Pick Your Own Fruits and Vegetables and Savor the Harvest at the Cherry Pie Café.

She dismounted from the motorcycle and removed her helmet. Marc had turned off the engine in a gravel turnabout featuring signs in the shape of pointing fingers. Cherry Orchards. Strawberry, Blueberry, Blackberry Picking. Peach, Plum and Apple Orchards. Lake Michigan, the Cherry Museum, Country Store, Restrooms and the Cherry Pie Café.

"Have you been here before?" she asked, grinning.

"Never," Marc replied. "But who can resist a place called the Cherry Pie Café?"

Mari pulled her tote bag out of the storage bin. "I'd like to change before we look around," she told Marc.

Marc also retrieved some folded clothes from the bin. He grabbed her hand and led her down a quaint path featuring bright flowers and a tiny bridge over a burbling stream.

Wearing a sundress, she came out of the bathroom

a few minutes later. She saw Marc standing at the entrance to the Cherry Museum. He'd changed into a pair of cargo shorts and a white, collarless shirt that made his bronzed skin glow in comparison. When he turned and looked at her as she approached, he broke into a wide grin, his teeth flashing in his sun-darkened face.

"What were the chances of *that?*" he drawled, staring at her sundress, patterned with red cherries.

She joined him in laughter until he reached out and grabbed her hand, leading her out into the gorgeous summer evening.

They picked up a little wooden basket from a receptacle and wandered into the cherry orchard. Again, they talked little, speaking with their eyes and small smiles, both of them comfortable in the silence as they filled the basket. Only the sound of a bee or two buzzing contentedly in the trees and the gulls calling in the distance reached Mari's ears. She idly wondered if the farm was deserted, because they saw no one. It was as if an enchantment had fallen over the place.

She quickly learned they weren't alone on the farm, however, when, their basket nearly overflowing with cherries, they exited the orchard. She glanced up at a clicking sound and saw a white-haired man wearing khaki shorts and white socks, taking their picture.

He was smiling when he lowered the camera a moment later.

"Hope you don't mind," he called. "I saw you while I was in the next grove over. You make quite a picture in that dress, ma'am. The photo would look great in my brochure." The man's kind eyes glanced over at Marc, and he nodded cordially. "With your permission, of course."

They approached the sunburned man and exchanged greetings and handshakes. As she suspected, he was the owner of the farm, a man by the name of Nathan McKinley. He told them that he and his wife had bought the farm last year and moved there from New York, looking for an escape from the city grind. It seemed right, somehow, she thought as she watched Nathan and Marc talk pleasantries, that the only person they'd conversed with during these golden hours was someone new to the area, a stranger to their past.

"You two should check out the café," Nathan said. "We have lake-view seating and the best cook in Harbor Country."

Marc glanced at her, his eyebrows cocked in a query. Mari nodded eagerly. She was in no mood to return to town at the moment. In fact, she wished this stolen day with Marc would never end.

They sat at one of the small tables in the cafe. Looking as large and picturesque as the Mediterranean Sea, Lake Michigan sparkled to their right. The only other occupant of the café was a brown dog whose tail wagged in friendly welcome when they sat, although he appeared to be too drowsy to move from his reclining position in the cool shade. The view was spectacular as the sun started to sink toward the lake, but Mari hardly noticed it. Her attention was all for the man who sat across from her.

The best cook in Harbor Country ended up being Nathan's smiling wife, Clarisse. Nathan's boasting about her cooking hadn't been without merit. Mari was surprised and pleased by the delicate, flavorful sauce on her Cornish hen, which was accompanied by mouthwatering mashed potatoes, garden-fresh steamed spinach and homemade cherry tarts. After Clarisse had cleared their empty plates, and Mari had requested a bag of the tarts and some homemade cherry salsa to take home, they lingered at their table, enjoying the view.

"I'm not surprised Nathan wanted to get a picture of you," Marc said after a while.

Noticing his warm gaze, she paused in sipping the remainder of her tea. "I know. How funny that I picked this dress to bring."

Marc reached across the table and covered her hand with his.

"I don't mean the dress," he said. "You're glowing, Mari."

"Am I?" she laughed, made a little self-conscious by his heady stare. "I got some sun today. We both did."

Marc shook his head, a small, quizzical smile on his lips. "It's not the tan."

Clarisse's arrival broke the delicate bubble of the intimate moment. Mari and Marc thanked Nathan and Clarisse profusely and promised to tell everyone who would listen about their wonderful farm and café.

A wistful sadness came over Mari as she climbed onto the motorcycle and Marc drove down the lane back to the main route. Night settled slowly on their return to Harbor Town.

She didn't know for sure what to expect when Marc pulled into her driveway. She released him reluctantly, having grown used to the convenient excuse of holding him so close while they were on the bike. He kept his feet planted on the concrete of the drive while she dismounted. Mari smoothed her dress and tried to read his expression, but his face was cast in shadow.

"I'm leaving the cherry tarts," she said as she removed her tote bag from the storage unit. "Give them to Brendan tomorrow at his party for me, will you?"

Marc turned the ignition on the motor and silence fell, interrupted only by the waves hitting the shore rhythmically on Sycamore Beach.

"Why don't you give them to him yourself? Come to his party with me."

Mari froze in the action of hoisting her bag to her shoulder. "What? No, Marc. Of course not."

"Why not?"

Her chest tightened when she heard the stiffness of his tone.

"It's a family party," she murmured. When he didn't reply, she continued. "Surely…surely your mother is going to be there?"

"She'll be there. What's that got to do with me asking you, as well?"

"Oh come on, Marc. It's got everything to do with it. I don't want my presence to ruin a family celebration."

"There's no reason your presence should ever ruin anything," he stated bluntly.

"But there *is*," Mari shot back. "There is, and you know it. It would be rude of me to show up and make your mother feel so uncomfortable at a family function. Excuse me for saying so, but it's disrespectful of you to suggest it."

He leaned toward her enough that she caught sight of the tightness of his lean jaw. "How do you figure that?" he demanded. His voice had been quiet enough, but she sensed his anger. The old, familiar feeling of helplessness rose in her.

"It's disrespectful and selfish to deliberately do something that would make Brigit unhappy."

"So I'm selfish for wanting to be with you."

"Yes. No," Mari sputtered. "I mean, it's selfish in this particular instance."

"What about this afternoon?" Marc replied briskly, reminding Mari all too well of his skills as a prosecutor. "My mother would have preferred I didn't spend it with you. Was I selfish then? My mother thought I should have worked things out with Sandra. I suppose I was selfish every time I went against her wishes, though. Right?"

"No, Of course not," Mari seethed. "That's not what I meant. This situation is different."

"I know it." His loud bark made her jump. "But that doesn't make it wrong for me to want to be with you."

She opened her mouth to make a blistering comment—how dare he try and make her seem like she was being petty for bringing this up?—when someone called her name. She blinked and peered through shadows thrown by the bushes lining the yard.

"Eric?" she called, thinking she recognized her friend's voice.

"Yeah," Eric replied. After a few seconds of silence, he stepped into the light of the streetlamp. He glanced warily from Mari's stiff expression to Marc's angry one.

"It was such a nice night, I thought I'd walk over and see how things went with the realtor today. Is everything okay?"

"Yes, of course," Mari replied quickly.

Eric's gaze flickered over to Marc. "Do you have some time to talk? I had some good news today. I've wanted to tell you about it all day, but I couldn't reach you on your cell."

"I...well, sure," she said, flustered by the turn of events.

She jumped when the motorcycle's engine suddenly roared in her ears.

"'Night," Marc said.

"Marc...*wait,*" she called as he began to turn the cycle around in the drive. She saw the tilt of his chin and suddenly knew for a fact that the golden day had come to an abrupt end.

Eric and she stood immobile, watching as Marc tore down the street in the opposite direction of the Kavanaugh house.

"Sorry. I didn't mean to interrupt," Eric said uncertainly. "It's just that I think I found the perfect manager for The Family Center today."

"Really? That's great."

"You don't seem as excited as I thought you'd be." He glanced down Sycamore Avenue. "Mari…are you *seeing* Marc Kavanaugh?"

Her spine stiffened at Eric's incredulous tone. She felt beleaguered and on edge, having her idyllic day with Marc end this way.

"Why do you ask it like *that?*" she bristled.

"It…it just seems a bit surprising."

"Does it really? It doesn't seem strange to me at all!" she said a little shrilly. Her emotions seemed to be reaching some sort of crescendo in her body. A strange, indefinable feeling had risen in her as she'd watched Marc ride away. She felt exhausted and yet prickly with adrenaline. She was vaguely queasy. In the back of her mind, she had the niggling thought that she was now hotly defending to Eric something she'd just been denying with Marc, and that upset her even more.

"Well… Cut me some slack, Mari, but yeah," Eric said slowly. "It does seem a little unusual, at the very least."

"Marc and I were involved years ago, before the crash. Maybe you didn't know that. Listen, Eric. I'm thrilled that you think you've found someone for the manager position. But I'm not feeling very well. You'll have to excuse me at the moment. I'm sorry."

"Mari, wait. Are you okay?"

She felt intensely guilty about treating a friend in such a fashion, but Mari couldn't seem to stop herself.

Eric's question went unanswered. She hurried up the front steps and into the darkened house. Without pausing to set her bag down, she rushed into the downstairs powder room and—much to her shock—threw up.

A moment later, she flushed the toilet and brushed her teeth. Leaning against the bathroom sink, she stared at herself in the mirror. A cold sweat had broken out all over her skin, and her face had gone pale beneath her tan. She started when she saw Eric's face appear behind her in the mirror.

"Mari?" he asked tensely.

"It's okay," she said shakily, noting his worried expression. She turned on the tap and filled her palm with cool water, then pressed it against her cheek. "I...I guess that bug is still bothering me."

"Seems like an awfully strange bug to me. I'm going to make an appointment for you with an internist I know at Harbor Town Memorial."

"No, Eric, that's not necessary."

"It *is*, Mari," Eric countered.

A trickle of unease went through her when she noticed how sober his expression was.

Chapter Six

Mari felt so good the next morning that she had herself convinced her illness last night had been the result of strong, conflicted emotion. Eric was kind enough to have arranged a lunch for her and Allison Trainor, the nurse he thought well-suited for the manager position of The Family Center. It had turned so hot and humid outside that they opted to eat indoors in the air-conditioning versus the sun-soaked terrace of the Captain and Crew Restaurant downtown.

"Your qualifications are exceptional," Mari mused as she perused Allison's resume for the tenth time.

Allison possessed both social work and nursing degrees and had significant managerial experience in hospitals and substance abuse rehab programs. Even better, Allison was not only warm and kind, but confident and down-to-earth.

Mari looked up as the waitress cleared the remains

of their lunch. "Eric says he knows of your work. So, as far as I'm concerned, the job is yours if you want it."

Allison looked pleased. "I accept. When Dr. Reyes told me about your plans for The Family Center, I was hooked. I like the idea of a treatment facility for people struggling with substance abuse combined with a place where family members can get education, understanding and support. What you plan puts a positive spin on a topic most people would rather ignore."

"I really want the emphasis to be on education for the community—clubs, workplaces, schools. Substance abuse is a community problem as well as an individual one. The stigma attached to it keeps us from seeing that."

"Agreed." Allison leaned back and gave a sigh of relief. "I wish all job interviews could be this easy."

Mari laughed. "Having people you trust make recommendations makes a big difference. Speaking of which, I don't suppose you have any recommendations for a clinician—someone to run educational, support groups and do individual therapy? He or she would also need to be comfortable giving public presentations."

"I do know someone. I don't know if she'll take the job, but she'd be perfect. Her name is Colleen Sinclair and she lives here in town."

"Colleen?"

"You know her?"

"Yes. We were friends...once," Mari said thoughtfully. "I wonder if she'd consider it."

"I can speak to her about it, if you like," Allison offered.

Mari remembered Colleen calling out to her at Jake's Place the other night. What had occurred next out in the parking lot had thrown a damper on any hope she'd had that she and Colleen might possibly resume their friendship.

Still… Mari thought the opportunity seemed too good to pass up without at least exploring the possibility. She wanted the best people working at The Family Center, and Colleen not only had the right credentials, she had the personal experience of dealing with the ramifications of substance abuse. Colleen was a survivor.

"I'd like to talk to her about it myself, actually. I happen to know she's busy with her son's birthday party today, but I'll try and contact her tomorrow."

Allison had needed to hurry to get back to her current job at the hospital, so Mari was alone when she exited the bustling restaurant. The bright sun blinded her as she stepped from the dim interior.

A petite woman plowed into her. Both fumbled to stop a plastic container from falling on the sidewalk.

"It's all right. I've got—" The older woman stopped talking when she glanced up at Mari.

"Brigit." Mari blinked. She hadn't stood this close to her in years. Marc's mother had aged extremely well. Mari's tongue felt numb with shock. "I'm sorry. The sun blinded me there for a moment."

Mari nodded nervously at the container. "That must be Brendan's birthday cake. He and his sister came to visit me yesterday. They're such lovely children—"

Abruptly, Brigit stepped around her and marched away without another word, her spine ramrod straight.

Ice poured into Mari's veins. She stood there on sunny, muggy Main Street, her skin tingling and her limbs starting to tremble. The unexpected encounter with Brigit Kavanaugh had a profound effect. She'd dreaded running into her, and now she had…in the literal sense.

In Mari's younger years, Brigit had always been so

warm toward her, so welcoming. Neither of Brigit's daughters had been interested in her hobby of wild-flower collection, but Mari had come to share Brigit's passion. They had gone on several jaunts together in the local meadows, searching for elusive flowers they'd earmarked in Brigit's *Wildflower Field Guide*.

Now, Brigit refused to speak with her and apparently loathed her, Mari thought as she recalled the cold, furious expression on Brigit's face. Having someone look at you with something akin to concentrated hatred wasn't an experience Mari was used to having.

Especially when that someone had once been a friend.

She sat down on one of the chairs outside Kate's Ice Cream Parlor for a moment until she regained her composure to walk back home. All the while, one thought kept circling in her mind.

Marc wanted me to attend that family party.

She stood and crossed Sutter Park. Children shouted gaily from the playground.

She should focus on what she needed to accomplish in Harbor Town. She should finish her mission and get out of here. It all made perfect sense.

Or at least she'd thought it did, until she climbed the steps to her house and made her habitual glance up Sycamore Avenue to the Kavanaugh house. The vision of Marc staring down at her as she awoke rose in her mind's eye.

I was thinking about all the nights I missed watching you while you slept.

Longing tore through her, so sharp it stole her breath.

Marc and Liam were the only two people remaining that evening after Colleen and Brigit took a horde of

Brendan's friends and Jenny to Kate's Ice Cream Parlor on Main Street. They sat at the kitchen table, covered with half a dozen pizza boxes, plastic cups, a half-eaten birthday cake, soda bottles and an array of toys and party favors. They'd volunteered to clean up, but neither brother seemed too anxious to get started.

"I've been wanting to talk to you about something," Marc said. "You've lost weight. You look like crap."

Liam scowled and scraped his fingers through his mussed, shoulder-length hair. "I've been too busy to work out lately. Or get a haircut. Not all of us have the leisurely schedule of a gentleman lawyer."

"I'm a government employee, not a fat cat. But that's not my point. You're working undercover again, aren't you?"

Liam's mouth turned hard. "Can't keep much from you, can I, counselor?"

Connecting the dots and not particularly liking the resulting picture, Marc just studied his brother for a moment.

"It's that corrupt cop investigation, isn't it?" Marc asked.

Liam raised his brows and slouched insouciantly in his chair, and Marc had his answer.

As the county's top prosecutor, Marc lived and breathed the same air as Chicago cops. He knew when something was up; he sensed when cops were jumpy.

"That inner ring of dirty cops is dangerous, Liam."

Blue eyes flashed. "You think I don't know that?"

"Just be careful. You'd put Mom in a grave if something happened to you. She's worried enough about Deidre."

"You have some nerve, accusing Deidre and me of being martyrs. Who do you think we learned it from, Mr. Defender of Victim's Rights?" Liam accused.

Marc didn't fall for the bait, just continued to hold Liam's stare until his brother sighed and glanced away.

"You sound like Mom. I told her I'd think about quitting the force when I'm done with this assignment, but not before. So the only thing I can do is tell you I'll be as careful as I always am. I don't have a death wish."

You sure as hell act like you do sometimes.

Marc bit his tongue to keep from saying the words out loud. He'd said enough for now. It wouldn't help things to start a fight with Liam.

Liam grimaced when he lifted his elbow off the table and saw that a miniature plastic hockey puck was stuck to his skin. "I guess we better start cleaning up," he mumbled.

"Right," Marc agreed unenthusiastically.

"They say we're in for a hell of a storm later on tonight," Liam said as he stood. He picked up the empty bag of cherry tarts Mari had donated for the party. "Hey…weird about you and Mari being back in town at the same time, huh?" Liam asked with affected casualness.

"Yeah," Marc replied shortly. He carried a stack of pizza boxes to the garbage.

"Marc."

He turned, something in Liam's tone making him cautious.

"I…I never told anyone. About the night of the accident. About Mari being at the house with you."

Marc narrowed his eyelids as memories of that fateful summer night assaulted him.

Liam's panicked shouts from downstairs had interrupted an intensely private moment between Mari and Marc fifteen years ago. In fact, they'd been about to make love for the first time as a storm brewed on the horizon. The news of the wreck had put a stop to that.

The crash had jolted Mari and him onto complete different life paths.

He was more than a little shocked at hearing Liam speak aloud about a topic that had been forbidden between them through some unspoken fraternal oath. Maybe it was Mari's presence in town, or maybe it was the threat of a storm in the thick air—the still, oppressive atmosphere not unlike that of the night of the crash—that had made Liam break the silence.

"It must have been rough, being with Mari that night," Liam said, his voice gruff, cautious.

Marc didn't reply, just resumed clearing the table.

Liam always had possessed a talent for bald understatement.

Mari kept herself busy that day by meeting the furniture deliverymen at The Family Center and arranging what items she could on her own. She'd dropped in on Natalie Reyes's accounting practice and spoken to Natalie about the status of the center's operating license and some other financial matters. They'd ended up chatting for hours. Natalie was one her favorite people—so quiet and reserved, yet so warm and giving once she accepted you into her private world. Mari knew Natalie rarely went out in public, self-conscious about the scarring on one side of her face. Mari had hoped her involvement in The Family Center would bring her out of her self-imposed confinement somewhat, but, so far, her friend remained shrouded.

Afterward, she returned to Sycamore Avenue where she spent the better part of the evening practicing her cello.

When she played, she entered a familiar, focused trance where she lost all sense of place and time. But, suddenly becoming aware of how hot it was, she paused to wipe sweat off her brow, change into a button-up, thin sundress, and open up a window in the bedroom, not that it helped to alleviate the stifling atmosphere. She resumed practice.

Isn't the air conditioner working? she wondered a little while later. She set her cello and bow aside and went downstairs to the thermostat.

"Do *not* tell me," she whispered in disbelief when the air conditioner didn't respond. In the distance, she heard thunder rumble ominously. She hadn't noticed a storm was approaching. With her air conditioner apparently on the fritz, she welcomed the prospect of relief from the oppressive heat and humidity.

She glanced at a clock. It was just past midnight. A feeling of sadness went through her. Now that the day was over, she realized that part of her had hoped Marc would seek her out following their bitter parting last night.

She walked out on the front porch. A warm wind swirled, causing the porch swing to jerk and sway. Some leaves skittered down the dark, deserted street, the sound striking her as hushed and furtive. She perched on the swing. Lightning flashed over Sycamore Avenue.

The weather reminded her of the night her parents had been killed. Funny how the realization didn't bring back the horror of rushing to the hospital and hearing her mother and father had been dead upon arrival. Instead, another memory flashed vividly into her mind: the hot, wondrous expression on Marc Kavanaugh's face when he'd looked down at her in his bed. She'd been naked and overwhelmed by desire.

Mari clenched her burning eyelids tight. Grief had wormed its way into that memory over the years, transforming it from a girl's gilded dream into a woman's tarnished regrets.

Tonight, the wonder of that moment had returned. She was so caught up in the poignant memory that she thought she'd imagined it when she heard Marc's voice.

"Mari."

She opened her eyes and spotted his shadowed form standing at the bottom of the stairs to the porch. The longing she'd experienced earlier that day swelled in her chest, making breathing difficult. For some reason, the fine hair on her arms and the back of her neck rose.

"Couldn't sleep, huh?" she asked quietly.

"Who could, on a night like this?"

Neither of them spoke as he came up the steps and sat several inches away from her on the swing.

"Hell of a storm brewing," he murmured as lightning lit up the street clear as day for a brief moment.

"Yeah," Mari replied shakily, wondering if he, too, thought of the similarity between this storm and that one so long ago. Thunder rumbled in the distance. "I'm glad about it. The air conditioner just went out. Hopefully the storm will break this humidity." She swallowed when he didn't reply. Was this what they'd stooped to? Talking about the weather? "How was Brendan's party?"

"He had a great time. He said to thank you for the tarts, by the way. He'd only share them with his best friend, Brian, much to Jenny's dismay."

She heard the smile in his voice and laughed. "I should have gotten a bag for her."

"I think she'll manage to survive on a week's worth of cake and ice cream," Marc said. "Are you interested in Eric Reyes?"

Mari started. She'd been lulled by his low, light tone. The switch in topic took her by surprise.

"Interested?"

"Yeah. Are you seeing him?"

"No...he's just a friend. A good friend."

She could only make out his shadow, but she saw him slowly nod his head.

"Ryan introduced me to him, years back. We've kept in contact, mostly by email over the years," Mari explained.

"Ryan must have met him during the lawsuit hearings."

"Yeah." A gust of wind caused the porch swing to shudder, despite Marc's firmly planted feet. She inhaled for courage. "I saw your mother downtown today."

"You did?"

"She didn't mention it?"

"No, she didn't. How did it go?"

"Not well," Mari replied with a mirthless chuckle. "When she realized it was me who'd bumped into her, she gave me the cold shoulder. Walked away without a word."

Marc cursed under his breath. "I'm sorry."

"It's not your fault," she said.

He didn't speak for a moment. Mari almost felt him examining her in the darkness.

"Is this your way of saying I told you so?" he finally asked with grim amusement.

She sighed and wiped the perspiration off her brow. "Maybe," she conceded. She fervently hoped to avoid another confrontation with him on the subject, but she wasn't going to apologize for what she'd said last night, either.

"Do you want me to take a look at the air conditioning?"

"Do you think you could actually fix it?" she asked, sitting up straighter.

"I'm not guaranteeing anything, but I can have a look. Let's start with the furnace, since it's inside, and it's about to start pouring. It might be the blower or a belt."

A thought struck Mari as she flipped on the hall light and led Marc to the closed doorway on the right.

"What's wrong?" he asked from behind her.

She glanced down at her skimpy dress and folded her arms over her breasts. In the darkness, she'd forgotten to think about how thin the fabric was. She turned her head warily. Her heart bumped against her breastbone at the vision of Marc in full light. He was wearing his customary beachwear—long cargo shorts that showed off his muscular, tanned calves and a blue T-shirt that picked up the color of his eyes. His dark blond hair had been sexily mussed by the whipping wind.

"Nothing is wrong." She waved at the shut door down the hallway. "The furnace is in the basement."

Her gaze shot away when she saw something flicker in Marc's eyes.

"Yeah. I remember that, strangely." His mouth quirked. "Lead the way."

Mari closed her eyelids briefly when she turned. She'd been so eager to have her AC fixed, she hadn't been thinking…

She flipped on the light over the basement stairs and took the squeaky steps at a brisk pace. She was proud that she didn't blush when she nodded at the furnace situated in a cubbyhole of the unfinished basement. Marc didn't say anything, just went over to it and opened the door that accessed the machinery. Mari stood back, admiring the flex and play of his muscles beneath the blue cotton.

Her heart seemed to skip a beat when he suddenly paused in his poking and walked into the narrow space between the furnace and wall. He opened up the breaker box and flipped a switch. When he returned, he saw humor dancing in his eyes.

"I used to kiss you back in that cubbyhole until my lips were chapped for days."

For a second, Mari's mouth just hung open. She was sure she must have imagined him saying it. She'd been a little embarrassed up in the hallway when she realized two things: one, she was wearing a thin, translucent dress with barely anything on beneath it, and two, she was about to take Marc to their first make-out hideaway. She'd thought he was tacitly agreeing to not make mention of the subject when he saw her discomfort. But here he'd just bluntly pointed out the elephant in the room.

Laughter burst from her throat. Her eyes sprung wide at the strength of her response, and she covered her mouth. She couldn't help it. It must be hysteria. When she saw Marc's grin widen, though, she wondered. How could the sound of Marc Kavanaugh's deep chuckle be anything but right?

"Remember that time when my mom came downstairs to put in a load of laundry while we were back there?" she asked between jags of laughter.

"Yeah," Marc replied as he opened the box he held. "We froze up for about two seconds and then got right back to the thick of things. I don't even remember when your mother went back upstairs again."

"Neither do I."

When she registered his altered expression and fading grin, the unexpected, swelling wave of amusement waned. Heat rose beneath her skin. Marc's gaze lowered to her breasts, which she'd exposed as she tried to cover her erupting laughter. He went still, masculine appreciation gleaming in his eyes.

Mari was a little surprised she couldn't hear the electricity popping in the air between them.

She cleared her throat and looped her arms beneath her breasts. When he met her gaze, she shook her head and rolled her eyes, attempting to package the poignant moment in the convenient mental container of silly childhood nostalgia.

But the moment *hadn't* evoked anything silly inside her. Far from it.

"You just threw a breaker. I reset it. The AC should work now," he said as he shut the door to the furnace.

"That's it?" Mari asked in amazement.

"I don't know. We'll have to go upstairs and see if the AC turns on or not."

She nodded, but neither of them moved. Instead they remained motionless, facing each other.

It felt like she was keeping a volcano of emotion from erupting from her chest. Her inhalation sounded ragged and raw in her own ears. It was really too damn much. Too much history. Too much *feeling*.

"Come here," Marc said, his voice quiet, but firm.

She flew across the room and into his open arms. A convulsion of emotion shuddered through her body and she gasped.

"Why do you fight it so much, Mari?" he asked gruffly as he stroked her back, trying to soothe her.

"I know it'll never work out." Tears shot out of her eyes with the same pressured intensity as her words. "But I can't seem to stop wanting you. Especially…"

His hand, spread on her lower back above her buttocks, paused. "What?"

"Especially tonight," she said, her face pressed against his chest. "You probably didn't notice, but the storm…the night…it's like—"

"The night of the crash," Marc whispered hoarsely.

Her heart seemed to swell at his words. So, he *had*

noticed the similarity of tonight to the one where their lives had been cleaved apart.

He put his fingers beneath her chin. He lifted her head until she looked up at him. She saw her own raw need reflected in his eyes.

He leaned down and caught a tear with firm, grazing lips. His eyes were open, watching…gauging her reaction as he rained kisses on her cheek and jaw, drying her tears, wetting his mouth with her sorrow. When he brushed his lips near the corner of her mouth, she turned to meet him.

She felt him stiffen as though an electric shock had gone through him when their lips touched. She sensed the steel edge of male desire that had leaped into his muscles. He softly sandwiched her lower lip between both of his own, parting her mouth, molding their lips together in a delicious kiss. Mari's eyes fluttered closed as a sensual languor weighted her limbs and heat expanded at her core.

She hungrily slicked the tip of her tongue along the seam of his mouth. A wild satisfaction tore through her when he groaned, deep and rough, and pulled her closer, pressing her tight to his body, taking her mouth in a possessive kiss.

Why was she doing this? She'd told him she wanted to be cautious. Yet here, in this moment, she felt nothing but glorious triumph that she'd inspired such a wholehearted, total response from Marc.

All his former tentativeness evaporated as he boldly explored her. Their flavors mingled, acting like an intoxicant on her brain. One hand clenched mindlessly at his T-shirt, while the other reached and knotted in the thick hair at the base of his skull. Her back arched as he leaned down over her and completely claimed her.

Both of his hands coasted up her back, simultaneously mapping her shape and stroking her.

He paused, both of his large hands spread across her ribs as though he held her heart in his hands. She moaned in rising need. He answered her call and caressed a breast. She moved back slightly, granting him more access. He sealed their wild kiss and lifted his head, watching her with blazing eyes, his nostrils slightly flared. He pressed an aching nipple to the center of his palm and closed his hand over her, gently kneading.

She felt his body tighten and harden in response to that intimate caress. It only fueled her mounting need. When he transferred his fingertips to the erect crest and gently charted the topography of her nipple through the thin fabric, desire ripped through her. She found herself jerking up his T-shirt, desperate for the sensation of his bare skin.

He made a rough sound in his throat. The next thing she knew he was lifting her in his arms. Lightning flashed in the dark, old house, and thunder answered in a ferocious roar. Neither of them spoke as he carried her up first one flight of stairs and then another. Words couldn't contain the fullness of that taut, burning anticipation, a powerful tension that demanded release.

Mari waved at the second door on the left—her old bedroom—her gaze never leaving Marc's.

Buffeted by the wind, the sheer curtains billowed inward when they entered the room. Marc laid her on the bed. When he straightened, Mari's hands flew to the buttons on her dress. He moved quickly, grabbing her wrists and halting her.

"No. I'm going to do it." His low, rough voice made goose bumps rise on her arms and her nipples tighten. "Just give me a second."

He began to undress. The light leaked in from the

downstairs hallway and allowed her to admire the sight of him as he went about his business with rapid efficiency. She was glad; she wanted him to hurry.

She didn't want logic to wriggle into her awareness. Not at this moment.

She knew Marc had shared her desire for haste when he began to strip out of his shoes and cargo shorts like he though his life depended on being naked. Her breath stuck in her lungs at the site of him standing and whipping his T-shirt off with a flex of lean, dense muscle. She eyed the shadow of light brown hair on his chest, following its trail to where it disappeared in his white boxer briefs.

"You're so beautiful."

He glanced up at her shaky whisper.

"No. You're the beautiful one," he said.

The dim light allowed her to see the feral glint in his eyes as his gaze traveled over the length of her. His haste seemed to mount, given the rapid manner in which he finished stripping. Mari glanced down when he stood before her. It hurt a little to look at him; he was so beautiful—proud and elementally male. The room flashed with brilliant white light, and thunder seemed to rattle the very air they breathed.

He sat on the bed next to her. Spellbound, Mari watched him. She couldn't draw breath as he unfastened her dress to the waist. He carefully peeled back the sides of the fabric, exposing her breasts. She convulsed with raw emotion when he just stared at her, his face intent, as though he wanted to take the image to his grave.

"*Hurry,* Marc," she whispered hoarsely.

His gaze leaped to hers, as if he'd caught her meaning. Who better to understand her desperation at that moment? Their joining had been interrupted fifteen years ago by news of mind-numbing loss.

But that was another night. Not this one.

His fingers moved fleetly at her plea. He drew the dress down over her legs then skimmed one hand down her buttock and thigh before reaching for her panties.

"I could never get over how soft you were," he muttered as he rid her of her underwear. She saw how rigid his face was as bent over her. "I always knew you were mine from the first time I touched you."

"Marc," she murmured desperately. Her desire almost hurt it was so strong. The night in Chicago had been wild, but this was a fiercer need that tore at her.

She cried out in protest when he didn't immediately press his weight against her but instead leaned over the side of the bed. He rustled for something in his shorts. She realized he was searching for a condom and experienced a brief moment of combined relief and guilt.

She hadn't even considered protection in the midst of her mindless need.

She watched, mesmerized as he sheathed himself. When he was done, she held up her arms, beckoning him.

He lowered himself. She sighed in relief at his weight pressing against her. His dense muscles were a sensual blessing pressed to her soft breasts, his arousal brushing against her belly and the juncture of her thighs.

She ran her hands over smooth skin encasing dense muscle and bone and opened herself to him. His mouth covered hers possessively as he entered her, her ecstatic cry muffled by thunder.

Rain began to pound on the roof and earth. The elm tree outside her bedroom window thrashed against the side of the house. But that storm was nothing compared to the one happening in Mari's body as Marc slowly staked his claim.

When he was fully sheathed in her, he dropped his

forehead on the pillow next to her cheek, his rib cage heaving. A great tenderness penetrated her arousal. He was the strongest man she knew—male virility personified—but in that moment, he was as helpless with his desire as she was. She caressed his shoulder and ran her fingers in into his hair.

"It's okay, Marc. It's okay."

He rose over her, his facial muscles tight and straining. "I don't know if I can control it," he warned in a choked voice.

"Then don't try."

He started to move.

She understood him perfectly. She existed at the eye of this storm with him. She clenched her teeth tight as her nerve endings began to fire madly with signals of sensual friction, making her want to purr and scream at once. He slaked himself—demanding and forceful—but she met him for every deep, driving thrust, an equal partner in this greedy consumption, both of them seemingly rushing toward the finish line to assure themselves the moment wouldn't be ripped away from them as it had in the past.

The headboard began to clack rhythmically against the wall. Their bodies became glazed with sweat as they both raced for that treasure, grasping blindly for it, requiring it like they required that next gasp for air. Marc reached it first. She held him at her core, knowing she'd forever remember him throbbing deep within her and the poignancy of his rough groan as ecstasy ripped through him. Still in the midst of his climax, he reached between their bodies, finding her most sensitive flesh… demanding she join him in that sweet conflagration.

Her back arched as she followed Marc's silent demand and she shook in a storm of release.

Chapter Seven

Marc propped himself up on his forearms, his neck bent as he fought to catch his breath.

He lowered his head to Mari's and pressed his mouth to her neck, absorbing her movements as she gasped for air. After a moment, he lifted his head. Her breasts heaved as she panted. Her large, liquid eyes were open, watching him.

He glanced down over her face, neck and elegant, sloping shoulders. Had he really just made love to this exquisite woman with all the finesse of a steam engine going at full throttle? He couldn't regret it. His need for total possession had been as easily controlled as the storm that raged outside the window. His gaze lingered on the pale globes of her breasts rising and falling. The delicate nipples were still stiff from desire.

He lowered and kissed the tip, lingering to feel her texture against his sensitive lips. He felt himself lurch in the tight embrace of Mari's body and realized he was segueing rapidly from satiation to arousal again.

"I know you wanted to go slowly, but it wasn't something I could control," he whispered roughly near her breast.

He lifted his head. Lightning illuminated the room, allowing him to see the shadow of uncertainty falling across her delicate features.

He sighed. "I'd better..."

He shifted his hips, letting his actions finish his sentence. Leaving Mari's warm, tight embrace made him grimace. He wasn't ready to withdraw.

Not even close.

"I'll be right back," he told her before he walked into the hallway.

His memory served him in his search for the bathroom. He was once allowed to come upstairs in the Itani summer house when they were little. He and Ryan had been friends, and they had occasionally condescended to hang out with their little sisters, Colleen and Mari.

Until the summer after Mari's freshman year of high school.

Kassim and Shada Itani had apparently noticed the way Marc stared at their blooming, beautiful daughter, and the rules in the Itani household had changed drastically.

Marc had never really thought much about the Itani's ethnicity and religion before that summer. But when Mari had become a young woman, Marc was forced for the first time to realize the vast differences in their backgrounds and culture. He could still recall how stunned he was when he learned how rigidly Mari's dating would be monitored by her parents. They were nowhere near as strict with Ryan.

It quickly became clear to Marc that under *no* circumstances would Mari be allowed to date an Irish-American boy from a liberal, Catholic family. He may have been acceptable as Ryan's friend, but, when it came to Mari, he was a pariah in Kassim and Shada Itani's eyes. Their grins of delight upon seeing him subtly changed over a single summer, replaced by tense, slightly suspicious expressions.

Of course, he and Mari had seen each other, anyway. Not much could stand in the way of two determined teenagers with hormones raging through their blood. Whenever and however they could manage to be together, they did it.

He washed his hands. Thinking about all the tenuousness of being with Mari when they were kids made him anxious to return to her. Would it always be that way? Not if he had his say about it.

He impatiently swiped his wet hands on a hand towel and hurried into the stuffy hallway. Before he joined Mari in the bedroom, he hurried downstairs and flipped the gauge on the thermostat. The AC hummed to life.

"Success," he proclaimed as he entered the room.

"Cocky," she murmured.

She snorted when he plopped down next to her, making the mattress squeak in protest, and immediately began to ravish her neck. He liked the sound of her laughter so much he tickled her with his whiskers.

"Is that a complaint?" he growled between tickles and nibbling her neck. He couldn't get enough of her taste on his tongue.

"Oh no…heaven forbid I'd complain about *that*."

Marc raised his head, grinning. He glanced down, realizing for the first time that Mari had drawn the sheet over her nakedness. He raised his eyebrows, his mirth fading. She stopped laughing, as well, when he tugged the sheet to her thighs. He sobered at the vision of her beauty.

"Please don't hide yourself from me anymore."

He opened his palm along the side of her ribs and stroked her from breast to thigh, awed by how she flowed beneath his hand like warm silk. He met her eyes. Her expression had become as somber as his.

"All right," she acquiesced quietly. "For tonight."

He leaned down and kissed her abdomen. Her taut muscles leaped beneath his lips. Relishing the delicate shivers he evoked from her flesh, he lowered his mouth, exploring the sensitive skin of her lower belly. He wasn't above pressing his advantage.

"Not just for tonight, Mari," he corrected. He skimmed his lips against the satin skin of her inner thigh, and she opened for him with a sigh. "Not ever," he murmured before he lowered his head.

Mari awoke the next morning to the sound of her cell phone ringing in her purse. She opened her eyes. The sunlight streaming through the window was so intense, she had to squint.

She squeaked in panic and raised her head.

"What's wrong?" Marc asked groggily.

For two seconds, Mari just stared incredulously at him. The vision of him—naked, sleep-rumpled and sexy as hell—seemed to score her consciousness. She lay in the circle of his arms. Her head had been resting on his chest. Everything came back to her in a rush: the storm that had raged outside of the house and inside of the bedroom, as well, the sensual hours of making love throughout the night, the complete focus on one another as they tried to get their fill…

Never fully succeeding.

Mari glanced over at Marc's mouth and the succulent flesh of dense pectoral and shoulder muscles.

"It looks like it's late, and I have an appointment at the hospital at nine-thirty, not to mention a ton of other things I need to do today," Mari said.

The drowsy look in Marc's blue eyes evaporated.

"What's wrong? Why do you have a doctor's appointment," he demanded.

"It's nothing," she murmured. She touched his upper arm as a signal to warn him that she was getting out of bed, but instead, she lingered, caressing his bulging biceps with appreciative fingertips. "I've been struggling with a little bug ever since the plane trip from San Fran to Detroit," she said, sighing when she felt Marc's fingers at the back of her scalp.

"You don't seem sick to me."

His low rumble caused her to open her heavy eyelids, which had uncooperatively drifted closed under the influence of Marc's massage.

"I agree. I'm fine. I'm just doing it to humor Eric," she whispered.

His hand ceased moving.

"Reyes?"

Mari blinked. "Yes," she said hesitantly, taking in Marc's stiff features. "He saw me get sick the other night and made a big deal about making an appointment for me. He's a doctor, you know."

"Yeah. I know."

Her mouth fell open but nothing came out. She knew that both Eric and Natalie had used the money from the lawsuit to get educations and improve their prospects. Their mother had come from Puerto Rico years back with little more than the clothing on her back. She'd worked for eighteen hours a day as a maid in various locales to support her two children. Miriam Reyes had drilled the importance of education in her children's heads.

Mari admired Natalie and Eric for what they'd done after their mother had been killed in the crash. How many people won lawsuits only to throw away the money on foolish schemes or unneeded luxuries? Not the Reyes. Instead, they had carefully planned futures for themselves, keeping in mind what their mother would have wanted for her children. No one could replace a loved one with money, but being careful about what was done with that money made a difference.

It did to Mari, anyway.

She swallowed as she glanced at Marc. "So...you found out that the Reyeses used the lawsuit money to get educations. Eric became a surgeon and Nat is an accountant," she said quietly.

"I didn't know—not until the other day," he replied.

"Oh. I...I wonder..."

"What?" Marc asked.

"If...if you ever wonder what I did with my share of the lawsuit money?" She studied the pillowcase. The ensuing silence seemed to ring in her ears.

"Yeah. I've wondered," he finally said.

"I want to tell you about it," she whispered. "It's the main reason I came back to Harbor Town."

He looked puzzled, but his long, stroking fingers resumed their sensual massage.

"When do you want to tell me about it?" he asked.

"How about tonight at dinner? I'll make you something here at the house," she suggested. Mari couldn't help but become preoccupied by his narrowed gaze on her mouth.

"How about if we make love right now, and you tell

me after that?" he suggested. He grasped her shoulders and gently pulled her up several inches. Mari moaned softly at the sensation of their naked skin sliding sensually together. The hand at the back of her head pushed her down to his mouth.

"Oh…that'd be…I…" Mari mumbled incoherently between Marc's kisses. "Marc…I can't…doctor's… appointment."

He leaned back. His smile was part angel and part devil. Mari couldn't fathom how he managed to pull it off.

"Nothing else but your health could make me stop," he said silkily.

Mari snorted doubtfully. He turned on his side, rested his hand and watched her while she grabbed a robe out of the closet. She glanced up and caught him staring at her breasts as she covered them. He sighed and lay on his back, his gaze on the ceiling.

"It's going to be a long wait until suppertime," he said dolefully.

She chuckled and started out of the room to take a shower.

"Mari?" he murmured, all traces of mock sadness gone from his voice.

"Yes?" she asked, turning.

"You'll call me if anything is wrong, as far as the doctor?"

"Nothing is going to be wrong," she said, smiling. She saw his raised brows and nodded her head. "Yes, I'll be sure to call in the rare event I have a dire illness."

"Just call me. Period," he said.

She nodded, hesitant to yank her eyes off the glorious vision of him propped up on the pillows and naked save for a thin sheet draped low on his hips. She shook her head as if to ward off his spell and exited the room.

It was hard to think like a rational human being with Marc around.

Once she reached the hospital, Mari noticed she'd missed a call from her brother. She put off returning his call, none too eager to speak with him when memories of Marc still crowded her consciousness. Instead, she called the number Allison had given her yesterday for Colleen, Marc's sister. She still clung onto the strand of hope that Colleen would at least meet with her to discuss The Family Center and a possible job.

Colleen didn't answer, but Mari left a message with her number saying she'd love to meet while she was in town if she had a chance. If she didn't call back, at least Mari would have her answer.

Eric had made her appointment at Harbor Town Memorial with a friendly, middle-aged, female physician named Estelle Hardy. She kept up such a pleasant, steady stream of conversation while she examined Mari that it hardly felt like a typical doctor's visit. She sent her to the lab and asked her to sit down in the waiting room until the results could be obtained. While she was waiting, Mari saw with a leap of excitement that Colleen had returned her call. Colleen had left a warm message, saying that she very much wanted to meet and could stop by Mari's house after work that afternoon, if it was convenient.

Mari immediately redialed Colleen's number. She got her voice mail at the same time that Dr. Hardy's nurse beckoned to her. Mari left another message saying she'd be happy to have Colleen over at the house at five, as the nurse led her to a consulting room.

She was just ending the call when Dr. Hardy walked in, carrying a chart.

"Well, I think we've figured out the reason for your malaise and bouts of nausea," Dr. Hardy said after they'd both sat down.

"Really? What?" Mari asked, still happily preoccupied with the prospect of Colleen Kavanaugh agreeing to see her again.

"You're pregnant, Mari."

Chapter Eight

Through the roar in her ears, Mari distantly became aware of a familiar voice. She blinked open her eyes with effort. Eric Reyes sounded nervous.

"Mari? Mari...open your eyes, please."

She saw him standing in the consulting room. He looked very doctorlike in an unbuttoned lab coat and with a stethoscope around his neck. He also looked very, very worried, Mari realized. She abruptly sat up on the exam table.

"What's wrong, Eric?" she demanded.

A bewildered, alarmed expression came over his handsome features. He reached out, stilling her from sitting up farther.

"What's wrong with *me?*" he asked dubiously.

She just stared at him, amazed. Disoriented.

"You passed out. Estelle Hardy called me down here. She knows we're friends. Mari, what the hell is wrong?

Estelle refused to tell me—patient confidentiality and all."

For a few seconds, she just stared at him, her mouth hanging open, the news Dr. Hardy had given her minutes ago striking her consciousness like a hammering blow.

"I'm pregnant," she blurted before she could stop herself. She wasn't telling him as much as repeating the shocking news to herself.

"You…you are?" She blinked and looked up into Eric's face. "It's…that's…wow," Eric finished feebly. He inhaled slowly, collecting himself. "I was beginning to wonder, given your symptoms."

"You were?" Mari asked. "Why didn't you say something?"

He shrugged helplessly. "I thought it seemed a little farfetched after you'd told me about breaking up with James five months ago," he said, referring to Mari's old boyfriend.

"James?" Mari repeated dully as if she'd never heard the name in her life.

"Yeah. *James Henry.* The guy you saw for four years?" Eric's grip tightened on her arm. "Mari, I think you need to lie down again. You're white as a sheet."

"No, no, I'm fine," she mumbled. She realized that she was just blankly staring at Eric's face again. It occurred to her he must be wondering who the father was—

Bewildering flashes of images, memories and feelings flooded her awareness, making it difficult for her to concentrate. She saw Marc standing there just inside the revolving doors of the Palmer House Hotel in Chicago, the sight of him striking her as thrilling and sad at once—thrilling, because he'd grown into such a beautiful man, just as she'd known he would; sad, because all evidence of the boy she'd once known was gone forever.

She recalled Marc's fierce, focused lovemaking last night, heard his husky voice.

Not just for tonight, Mari.

Another thought kept buzzing around her consciousness like a persistent fly.

This child was the grandchild of her parents—and of the man who had killed them.

She winced when another thought struck her as she slowly, carefully started to get off the examining table.

Not to mention that the only living grandparent would want nothing to do with my baby.

Mari operated on autopilot for the rest of the day. She straightened up the house for a showing at noon, then stopped by Natalie Reyes' office to pick up the employment contract for Allison Trainor. While she was there, she made an abbreviated copy of the contract so that she could show it to Colleen this afternoon, in case she was interested in the position.

She recalled while driving down Vista Pointe Drive that she'd told Marc she'd make dinner for him that night.

A wave of panic rose in her. She pulled the car over to the side of the road, put the vehicle in park and instinctively placed her hand on her belly in a protective gesture.

"I'm going to have a baby," she said out loud, needing to hear it, needing to let it seep into her consciousness. It didn't help much. Everything that had happened since the thunderstorm last night to the present moment had a surreal cast to it.

After she'd recovered from her faint this morning,

she'd actually sat down and had a discussion with the doctor. Dr. Hardy had made a recommendation for an obstetrician at Harbor Town Memorial, and her nurse had scheduled an appointment for Mari the following week. The information and advice Dr. Hardy had offered hadn't seemed to help pound the strange new reality into her brain, though.

It must be shock, Mari thought as she proceeded down the street again.

On the way home from the grocery store, she noticed she'd missed another call from her brother. She didn't call back. She didn't know if she could bear talking to Ryan when she carried such a volatile secret.

An hour's practice on her cello temporarily quieted the nagging, persistent question—*what am I going to do?*

In the shower, she examined her abdomen carefully, but there was no sign on the surface, anyway, of the miracle occurring in her body. A wondrous excitement rose up in her, and for a few seconds, she had a wild urge to run down the street and charge into the Kavanaugh house to share the news with Marc.

Reality sobered her quick enough, however. She finished showering, blow-dried her hair and dressed in a tangerine-colored linen skirt and matching tunic. She added a leather belt and slid into her favorite brown sandals.

She made some advanced preparations for a dinner she was both dreading and anticipating. Should she call Marc and cancel? It was going to be bad enough acting like she hadn't received earth-shattering news this morning in front of Colleen Kavanaugh, but how could she look at Marc and not blurt out the truth?

Her feelings continued to run the gamut from dread to excitement, numbness to exhilaration. It was crazy.

Mari supposed all the things she'd heard about pregnant women and their out-of-control emotions must be true. She was living proof.

At a quarter to five that afternoon, Mari heard a knock. She put the pitcher of herbal iced tea she'd just prepared into the refrigerator and hurried to the front door. Colleen stood on the porch wearing a pink sundress that showed off her golden tan. She smiled when Mari opened the screen door.

"I would have never thought you could get prettier than when you were eighteen, but I see you've gone and done the impossible."

"I could say the same for you." Mari laughed suddenly and shook her head, overwhelmed with happiness at seeing her old friend again. She waved Colleen inside. "Come in! I'm so pleased you—"

She paused when she saw Colleen glance worriedly toward the Kavanaugh house. "I was about to tell you, I ran over to ask if we could meet at my mother's? I was in the process of dropping Jenny off so Mom could watch her, but Mom's friend Mrs. Aichman called and asked if Mom could take her for her doctor's appointment. I would have just brought Jenny along, but she fell asleep at Mom's. She came down with a cold—it's kept her up for the past two nights—and I hate to wake her. She really needs the sleep. So that's why I'm here early."

Colleen faded in her pressured explanation. Her eyes sharpened on Mari's face.

"I can guess what you're thinking, Mari," Colleen said quietly. "No one else is home. Marc and Liam took Brendan to the beach this afternoon, and I doubt they'll be back for a while. And like I said, my mom just left to run Mrs. Aichman to the hospital."

Mari smiled, trying to hide her nervousness at the idea of stepping into the Kavanaugh house when she was quite sure she wouldn't be welcomed there by the owner.

"I completely understand about Jenny. Why don't we just reschedule our appointment?"

"Appointment?" Colleen said, blue-green eyes going wide. "You make it sound so official. I thought it was just a reacquaintance chat between two old friends."

Two old friends.

"If you're sure it'll be all right—"

"It'll be fine," Colleen assured. "Come on. Let's go catch up on the last fifteen years of our lives."

That's precisely what they attempted to do while sitting on the Kavanaugh's front porch sipping iced lemonade. Mari was having such a nice time chatting with Colleen that she realized an hour had passed, and she'd hardly worried about the news she'd received that morning. She also hadn't spoken to Colleen about The Family Center. She rectified that as soon as she made the realization.

Colleen listened, a sober expression settling slowly on her face as she listened to Mari try and put into words her plans for the money she'd received from the lawsuit so many years ago.

"You never touched any of that money?" Colleen asked in a hushed tone after Mari had talked nonstop for several minutes.

Mari shook her head. "You'll never know…" she began, pausing when her throat tightened uncooperatively. "You'll never know how many times I wondered what that money had been meant for before the lawsuit. Had it been saved for your college funds? Marc's law school? For Deidre's and your weddings, perhaps? Nest eggs for Kavanaugh grandchildren?" She met Colleen's stare and smiled despite the tear that had fallen down her cheek. "It was torture to consider it. I had loved all of you, in a way. I considered just giving my portion back—"

"No," Colleen quietly interrupted. "That wouldn't have been right. It would have offset the balance of things."

Mari's mouth fell open, stunned that Colleen had captured so succinctly the essence of her feelings.

Colleen stared at the glass of lemonade in her hand with a fierce focus.

"I accept the job offer," she said.

"You…you do?" Mari asked, surprised at her decisiveness.

Colleen nodded. "I'll look over the contract, of course. I'm not sure how much notice will be required at my current job, but yes—I want to do it." She glanced over at Mari and smiled. "It seems right somehow, you starting The Family Center and me working there. Like coming full circle."

Mari inhaled and laughed shakily.

"What?" Colleen asked.

"I'd forgotten how formidable you can be at times."

Colleen made a face. "Doesn't go with the blond hair, huh?"

They both laughed.

"There's one other thing you should know, Colleen, before you make your final decision."

"What?"

"Eric Reyes will be working at the Center, as well."

Colleen's amusement faded. "In a full-time capacity?" she asked.

"No, no," Mari assured. "He'll only be volunteering an afternoon or morning every week, but, given what happened in the parking lot the other night, I thought I should mention it."

"I see." She seemed to consider. "Well, I can get past it if he can. We don't have to be best friends to work together for a few hours a week."

Mari sighed with relief.

She caught movement out of the corner of her eye and saw Marc's car coming up Sycamore Avenue. Colleen's glance followed Mari's.

"I'm sorry, Mari," Colleen said.

She gave Colleen a smile of reassurance. Of course, Colleen didn't know what had been happening between her older brother and Mari, but she must have sensed the tension.

"It's okay," Mari assured her. "I was making dinner for Marc tonight, anyway."

"You were?" Colleen asked. She seemed pleased.

A moment later, Brendan bounded up the porch steps wearing swim trunks, flip-flops and a towel around his neck.

"Uncle Liam dared Uncle Marc to do a back somersault off the dunes, and he *did* it!" Brendan told his mom in a rush of excitement. He noticed Mari sitting next to his mother and said a polite hello before he launched into a description of his uncle's dive.

"Marc," Colleen scolded as her brothers came up the steps. "You're going to hurt yourself. You're too old to be doing stuff like that."

"That's what Liam thought," Marc replied. His cocky grin at his brother froze when he saw Mari sitting there.

She realized he hadn't noticed her because of the porch railings. Mari tried to look calm, but suspected she failed awfully. He was wearing a pair of board shorts, a white T-shirt and a pair of sunglasses. For just a few seconds, the man and the boy of her memories blended seamlessly.

"Hey, Mari," Liam greeted her pleasantly, as if it was the most natural thing in the world for them to find her there. "You should have come with us. Marc could have pulled off a double if you'd been watching."

He flinched and laughed when Marc flicked his towel at his calf.

"What?" Liam asked his brother, eyes wide with innocence. "That's the way it always worked, wasn't it? Mari Itani comes around, and Marc suddenly has to double anything he's doing…dive twice as high, swim twice as fast, flirt twice as much…"

"Tackle his brother twice as hard," Marc muttered under his breath as he came the rest of the way up the stairs.

"Man," Brendan muttered in awe as he looked at Mari. "You *should* come with us next time, Mari."

Colleen snorted, but Marc seemed to have forgotten Liam's teasing as he leaned against the rail, his arms loosely crossed, his stare on Mari.

"What are you doing here?"

"Catching up," Mari replied, nodding toward Colleen.

Marc nodded slowly, his laserlike gaze never wavering from her. "You never called me today."

"Oh…" She furtively glanced over at Colleen and Liam, suddenly feeling like she and Marc were in a spotlight on a stage. "I…I forgot."

His eyebrows arched. "Not about dinner, too, I hope."

"No," she replied, trying to be nonchalant. It was difficult with not only Liam and Colleen, but Brendan watching their exchange with apparent interest. Mari wondered if Brendan thought his uncle was going to do a double somersault from the porch to the front yard. "I went shopping earlier and have some salmon marinating in the fridge."

Liam clapped his hands together loudly. "Great. I love salmon."

"Shut up, Liam," Colleen said without heat.

Mari was staring at Marc and laughing when a vehicle pulled into the drive. She recognized Brigit behind the wheel and hopped up from her sitting position like she was on springs. She'd been enjoying herself so much she'd forgotten the time.

"I should be going," she said as she hurried toward the stairs.

Both Colleen and Marc called out to her. Ignoring them, she rushed down the steps. She realized she'd stood up too abruptly. It seemed as if she was walking underwater as she made her way down the sidewalk. Her sense of unreality only deepened when she heard a man's voice coming from down the street.

She knew that voice.

She peered at her house. Wearing jeans and a dark red T-shirt, her brother Ryan stood next to a blue car. He stared back. Even at this distance, she sensed his surprise…his shock. Her feet slowed. Her vision blurred.

Oh no…*not* again…not *now,* she thought in dazed irritation, recognizing the symptoms from this morning in Dr. Hardy's office.

Suddenly, a pair of arms encircled her from the back. Somehow, despite her disorientation, she knew it was Marc. She didn't resist when he took most of her weight and leaned her body back against the length of him.

"It's okay, Mari. I've got you. Take a some nice, easy breaths," Marc's voice rumbled near her ear.

She did what he said and soon the green canopy of the giant sycamore tree overhead resolved into separate, rustling leaves.

"I'm okay," she murmured. She tried to straighten and resume her flight from the Kavanaugh house. Marc allowed her to take her weight back on her feet, but he refused to move the circle of his arms from around her waist. In her new, upright position, she could see directly in front of her.

What she saw made her wish she'd passed out.

Brigit Kavanaugh stood to her right, her face pale and stony as she stared at them. To the left, her brother Ryan stalked down the sidewalk toward the scene. Despite her disorientation, she was so happy to see him. He was safe. Ryan was home. She gave a soft moan when she saw Eric Reyes jog up behind Ryan. She realized it was Eric's car her brother had stood next to a moment ago.

"Ryan? What are you doing here?" she asked through numb lips. She still wasn't entirely convinced she wasn't hallucinating.

Her brother's mouth was clamped tight in a straight line.

"I got sent home early," Ryan said stiffly. "I'll explain later. Let's get you home."

Out of the corner of her vision, she saw Brigit walk past them. Most of her attention was on her brother's fixed, furious expression as he looked over Mari's shoulder. She felt Marc's arms stiffen around her waist when Ryan reached toward her.

"Come on, Mari," Ryan said, never removing his gaze from the man who held her.

"Let go of her this instant, Marc. I don't want them here," Mari heard Brigit say behind them.

"You heard her," Ryan said in such a soft, deadly tone that Mari doubted anyone else heard him.

Still, Marc showed no signs of relaxing his hold. If anything, it seemed as if his arms hardened into steel bands.

"Mari?" she heard Marc ask from behind her.

"It's okay." She twisted until she caught a glimpse of his face. He looked every bit as tense and angry as Ryan. Every bit as dangerous, too.

"I said, *let* go," Ryan seethed.

Fear swept through her when she saw the blazing look of anger in Marc's eyes.

"I'm all right. Let go, Marc. *Please*," she implored before he said something volatile and this whole keg of gunpowder exploded in their faces.

Marc's gaze flickered to her face. His arms slowly loosened around her.

Mari turned toward him and whispered without meeting Marc's eyes. "Maybe…maybe we ought to cancel for tonight."

Ryan grasped her hand and led her down the Kavanaugh's front walk, Eric joining them at the boundary of the Kavanaugh yard. She glanced back furtively as they reached the sidewalk. Looking young and bewildered, Brendan stood on the front steps. Brigit, Colleen and Liam Kavanaugh formed a semi-circle around Marc. Brigit appeared angry, Colleen and Liam tense.

Mari turned away. She didn't want to interpret the expression on Marc's face as he watched her walk away with Ryan and Eric on either side of her.

Chapter Nine

Mari glanced up after dinner that evening when her brother walked onto the shadow-draped terrace at the back of their house.

When they'd first arrived, Ryan had suggested that Mari go upstairs and rest following her episode of dizziness. Mari had insisted she wasn't an invalid, and that she wasn't going to go lay down when her brother was just returning home from a yearlong tour of duty in Afghanistan. She scolded him for not giving her warning about his early release, but Ryan said he'd wanted to surprise her. Apparently he and Eric—who were correspondents—had been conspiring over the matter. Ryan had wanted to return to Harbor Town to help Mari with The Family Center project. Her happiness at seeing Ryan home and healthy did a lot to ease her disappointment about what had happened at the Kavanaughs, but a sense of unease still lingered as her brother sat down across from her.

"It's strange to be back here, isn't it?" he murmured.

"Yeah, so many memories," she replied in a hushed tone.

A silence ensued. Ryan was six foot three inches tall, a hard-as-nails Air Force pilot, charming and courageous in equal measure. Nevertheless, Mari sensed how he hesitated to bring up the explosive topic of finding her in Marc Kavanaugh's arms. Mari had to admit, she was feeling uncertain around her brother, as well.

She suddenly regretted nothing more than blurting out that she was pregnant to Eric Reyes this morning. Had Eric told Ryan that volatile news on their drive to Harbor Town from the airport? If so, what conclusions was Ryan making? Mari could only imagine, as the news still didn't seem quite real to her, either.

Ryan nodded toward the overgrown trellis. "Dad's hydrangea finally took," he said.

Mari smiled in the darkness. "He fussed over that plant daily, remember? It looks like all it wanted was to be left alone," she said.

"Mari, what were you doing down at the Kavanaughs' house today?"

She blinked. Apparently memories of their father had dislodged the crucial question from Ryan's throat.

"I...I'd been visiting with Colleen. I've invited her to be the clinician and educator for The Family Center. She has excellent qualifications. She said yes." Enough light was leaking through the windows so that she could clearly see how tense Ryan's face had become. Mari slowly let out the air in her lungs. "I see you don't agree with my decision."

"I don't, but since when does that matter? I've always made it clear what I thought of you using all the lawsuit money for this. That money was meant for your future, Mari. Not for some philanthropic project."

"And yet you came," Mari challenged softly. She refused to start up their old disagreement now. What was the point? "You said you wanted to help."

"I do want to help. You. If it's important to you, then it's important to me."

"Thank you, Ryan."

"But I think it's a huge mistake to involve the Kavanaughs."

Mari sighed tiredly and her brother stirred.

"Forget about that damn Family Center and the Kavanaughs for the moment. Let's talk about you," Ryan said.

She glanced up warily. "Me? What about me?"

"Eric told me on the drive from Chicago that you haven't been feeling well. He said I should ask you about it."

"He…he didn't say anything else?"

"No. He didn't. But the moment I arrive in Harbor Town, the first thing I see is you running away from the Kavanaughs and nearly fainting in their front yard. What the hell is going on, Mari? Are you sick?"

"I'm fine. Really. I just… One second, Brigit Kavanaugh was pulling into the driveway and the next—"

Ryan leaned forward intently. "Has Mrs. Kavanaugh been giving you a hard time since you returned? She always did have a strong personality—"

"Ryan, let me finish," Mari interrupted sharply. Her brother clamped his mouth shut, but he still seemed agitated. Mari closed her eyes. This was the last thing she wanted. Ryan was her only living family. She hated the idea of arguing with him when she hadn't seen him for over a year. She was so thankful he was home and safe.

"What I was trying to say," Mari resumed in a quieter

voice, "is that I didn't plan on being, or want to be, at the Kavanaugh house when Brigit returned. I'd gotten up too abruptly from a sitting position, and then I looked down the street and saw you. The combination of all the things—the whole situation in general—made me a little dizzy, that's all."

"What about what Eric said?"

"Eric is worrying too much, Ryan," Mari said wearily. "This has been a whirlwind trip. I've had a lot to do."

"It's been too much for you. I'll take over the sale of the house. I can do anything you need done at the center, as well. Grass mowed, pictures hung, desks moved—I'm your guy."

Mari reached across the table and grabbed her brother's hand. "Thank you," she said earnestly. "You don't know how much that means to me, Ryan."

"Like I said. If it's important to you, I want to be here to help." Ryan's brow crinkled as he stared at her. "You look exhausted. Why don't you go to bed?"

"It's your first night back," Mari protested.

"I'm not going anywhere. At least not for a while. Not until the Air Force has decided I've had enough rest and relaxation and decides to ship me off again."

Dread settled in her belly like lead. "You've just completed your third tour. Surely they won't send you for a fourth?"

His dark eyes narrowed on her face. He seemed to regret his words. "Probably not, it just depends. One thing is for certain. I'm back for a long stretch, if not for good." He squeezed her hand. "Go on to bed. Come tomorrow, you can start ordering me around to do your grunt work."

Mari rolled her eyes and stood. Maybe Ryan was

right. She really did need some privacy to sort out her thoughts. She loved Ryan like crazy. How—and when— was she going to tell him that she was pregnant with Marc Kavanaugh's baby?

How and when was she going to tell *Marc,* for that matter?

She slowly went up the stairs to her bedroom feeling like the weight of the world was on her shoulders. She washed and brushed her teeth mechanically and remembered to take one of the prenatal vitamins Dr. Hardy had given her. When she got to her bedroom, she changed into a short, gold satin gown. The image of the Kavanaughs' tense faces as they stood in the front yard earlier suddenly rose in her mind's eye and caused a swooping sensation in her belly.

Maybe the wisest thing would be to say nothing to Marc at all. Was it really fair to subject a child to all the historical baggage and hurt that existed between their families?

The thought made her feel like two squeezing hands had wrapped around her throat.

She glanced at her bed. She envisioned their impassioned lovemaking last night. How fair was it to not tell Marc about his own child? She couldn't do that to him. She loved him too much.

Mari sat down heavily on the mattress and stared blankly into her open closet. It'd been the first time she'd admitted it to herself. Of course, she'd known she'd loved Marc once, but she'd been a girl…an infatuated, wide-eyed teenager. To acknowledge that the powerful force that throbbed in her breast at that moment was nothing less than the deep, passionate love of a grown woman shocked her to the core.

She was so stunned by her private admission that she was surprised to realize she had the capacity to be shocked even further. The branches on the old elm rustled in the stillness of the night, and Marc's face appeared outside her window.

"What in the world do you think you're doing?" Mari whispered when she'd opened the window.

She stepped back as Marc clambered across the sill. Marc tried to suppress his laughter when he met her stare. She'd looked poleaxed when she'd seen his face in the window.

"I couldn't think of how else to see you."

Mari made a repressive motion with her hand and walked over to a fan that sat on top of the dresser.

"For God's sake, why didn't you just knock on the front door?" Mari scolded him.

His amusement faded. He nodded significantly at the fan she'd turned on so that Ryan couldn't hear them speaking. "You really have to ask me that after what happened today?"

She placed her hands over her eyelids and sat on the edge of the bed. Guilt rushed through him when he realized how fragile she looked. His gaze lowered.

Fragile and beautiful. The little gown she wore left her smooth arms and legs bare and gifted him with the sight of her breasts pressed against very flimsy fabric. He yanked his eyes off the tempting sight of Mari sitting on a bed wearing next to nothing and tried to focus on what was important. She'd almost passed out cold on his mother's sidewalk today, and here he was gawking at her like a horny teenager.

He sat next to her on the bed. "I had to see if you were okay. I was worried."

"I'm fine," she said, sounding exasperated.

"You almost fainted today. What did you find out at the doctor's? Are you sick?"

He saw her throat convulse. "Dr. Hardy said I was perfectly healthy."

"Then why did you almost pass out?"

"Is it really that surprising?" she exclaimed, pulling her fingers away from her eyes and meeting his stare. "Your mother doesn't want me in her house any more than Ryan wants me to be there. This is a stupid, tangled-up mess and I can't believe I was so dumb as to put myself smack dab in the middle of it. I was an idiot to come back to this town!"

"You're not an idiot. You're compassionate and you're brave. I can't tell you how proud I am of you."

She just looked at him, her mouth gaping open in amazement. He resisted an urge to send his tongue through the tempting target of her lush, parted lips. He cleared his throat and forced himself to meet her incredulous stare. "Colleen told me about the center you plan to open for victims and survivors of substance abuse."

"She...she did?" Mari asked him slowly. "I wanted to be the one to tell you. I'm sorry."

He nodded. "Why didn't you tell me?"

"I was planning on doing just that, tonight at dinner," she whispered. "But then—"

"Ryan came home."

Mari nodded. When he saw how dull her usually brilliant eyes looked, he pulled her into his arms. She held herself stiff at first, but as he stroked her back, he felt her muscles begin to mold against his body. He didn't think she was crying, but he sensed she needed comforting, nonetheless. He felt a measure of satisfaction when her arms surrounded his waist.

It must have been a hell of a day for her.

Neither of them spoke for a minute or two, but he had never been more aware of another human being in

his life. He held her against him, all the while thinking
of her saving that lawsuit money got for all those years
and slowly coming up with the plan for The Family
Center.

He nuzzled her temple, inhaling the fresh, citrus scent
of her hair, urging her to lean back and look at him. She
complied. He stared down at her lovely face, glad to see
some of her typical vitality had returned to her eyes.

"All these years, I thought maybe you'd forgotten
Harbor Town."

"How could I ever forget this place?" she whispered.
"It was the place where I'd been the happiest I've ever
been in my life…and the saddest. It was the place where
I'd lost the most."

He kissed her softly. Her lips felt warm and respon-
sive beneath his.

"And you came back to try and make some sense
out of it all," he said next to her mouth a moment later.
"To give some purpose to a random, meaningless act
that should never have happened." He shook his head
slightly, still half in awe. "You're incredible, Mari."

"I'm not incredible. I'm beginning to think it was all
a mistake."

"No. It wasn't a mistake," Marc said steadfastly. "I
want to help you with it, if I can."

"You do?" she looked up at him, her golden-brown
eyes huge in her face.

"Does that surprise you?"

"No. Yes. A little." She bit at her lower lip. "Ryan
wants to help, too."

"Does he?" Marc asked, not paying as much attention as he should because he was still enthralled by the
vision of Mari's white teeth scraping across her damp,
plump lower lip. He blinked when he realized she was
staring at him, her brow arched in a query. "Oh," he

said as understanding dawned. "So you're foreseeing conflict between the Itanis and the Kavanaughs if we try to work together on this project."

"It did cross my mind."

"It could potentially be a land mine," Marc conceded after a moment.

"It seems like I've done nothing but navigate around a land mine since returning to Harbor Town," Mari admitted bitterly.

"Which brings me to the reason I climbed your tree tonight."

She gave him a wry glance. "I thought you did that because you're an idiot."

He smiled good-naturedly and flicked his eyebrows. "In addition to that. See, it struck me sometime today—maybe it was as your brother came to save you from the evil Kavanaughs—that you and I really need to get out of this town. Just for a few days," he added when she looked at him like he was crazy.

"Marc, I have a million things to do in order to get things started with the Center before I leave the week after next. The last thing I should be considering is leaving town."

"You just said that Ryan was going to help, and Colleen is on board now. Once Liam hears about the news, he'll likely volunteer some of his time. And I'm assuming Eric Reyes is involved in the project?"

Mari nodded doubtfully. "And his sister, Natalie. You remember her?"

Marc closed his eyes briefly and glanced away. He'd remember the young girl who'd been injured and scarred by the crash until the day he died.

"Of course I remember," he mumbled. "You're making my whole point, Mari."

"What do you mean?" she asked, obviously bewildered.

"You said you'd give this a chance," he murmured as he flicked his finger between them. "But *I* don't stand a chance with you while we're here in Harbor Town. There are too many obstacles. Too many memories. It's not a fair playing field."

"So what do you suggest?" she asked, looking wary.

"That you come to Chicago with me this weekend. Just for two nights," he added quickly when he saw her mouth open to argue. "There's nothing that can't be taken care of at The Family Center for a couple days without you."

"I can't, Marc!" she exclaimed. "Ryan just got home!"

"We won't be leaving for a few days, and you'll be back by Sunday," he reminded her. "Ryan is home for a while, isn't he?"

Mari nodded reluctantly.

When he sensed her wavering, he pulled out all his ammunition. He pressed his forehead against hers and kissed the end of her perfect nose. "Don't you think you owe it to yourself to get away from all the distractions for a period of time and just focus on us? Wouldn't you regret knowing that you'd never found out...*for sure?*"

She leaned back slightly, and he saw a world of doubt and longing in her eyes.

"I let you go once, because I thought I didn't have a choice," he whispered hoarsely. "I'm not willing to do that again. If you spend this time with me in Chicago, and you decide to walk away, I'll accept it. But I'm not willing to let you go this time until I know for sure you're certain, *absolutely* certain, that it's what you want. How else can you know that until you spend some time away with me, away from all the history of this town and the people? It's almost impossible to figure out here with everything and everyone around us."

He put his hand on the back of her head and tilted it forward, so that their foreheads once again met and their breaths mingled. Her long hair fell like a drape around them, increasing the sense of solemn intimacy.

"It's only fair, Mari."

"You always could talk me into anything," she whispered.

He smiled slowly.

"Don't be so cocky, Kavanaugh. I'm not so sure I'm happy about that fact," she added. "I can't seem to think straight around you."

"Come to Chicago with me," he entreated in a hoarse whisper.

She bit nervously at her lip. He waited on tenterhooks.

"Okay."

He seized her mouth with his own. He'd waited for that acquiescence. Now that he had it, he didn't bother to hide his hunger for her. She moaned softly when his tongue probed the sweet cavern of her mouth.

She sealed their torrid kiss a moment later, panting.

"Marc...if I go with you, you have to give me some space. I meant it when I said I can't think straight around you. I want to make a well-thought-out decision about whether or not we can have a future. I can't do that if you're always...doing that."

"Doing what?" he asked silkily as he plucked at her lips.

She joined him, despite her protestations, seeking out his mouth, sliding her tongue teasingly against his lower lip until he groaned and kissed her deeply once again. She tasted wonderful, like peppermint and woman and sex. He spread his hands over her satiny-smooth shoulders and pressed her down to the mattress. He came down over her, kissing her all the while, coaxing her until his body throbbed with a dull, insistent ache. Her breasts were a delicious, soft firmness against his ribs.

"This," Mari hissed a moment later against his mouth.

It took his lust-drunk brain a few seconds to understand what she meant. When he recalled their former conversation, he sighed and sat up, trying to ignore the tempting vision she made lying on the bed with her hair spread out around her and her breasts heaving beneath the thin, gold fabric.

She stood and tried to smooth her hair, which Marc had mussed with his fingertips. He watched her, scowling, as she went over to her closet and withdrew a robe. His frown only deepened when she covered herself. She was all serious business by the time she belted the garment with a defiant tug.

"I won't agree to go with you on this trip if you continue to do that, Marc."

"What? Do the most natural thing on earth?" he asked, trying to hide his irritation and failing.

"I'm serious," she said so loudly that he started. He narrowed his eyes on her. She looked desperate. "We both know we're sexually compatible. That's the easy part," she said, the stain on her cheeks deepening. "You brought up this proposition. If you truly want to discover if we have a future together, then we need to do more than…roll around in bed together."

His annoyance evaporated when he saw how nervously her hands moved over her belly. He sensed her fragility in that moment. "All right. If that's what you want, you've got it. I promise to follow your lead in regard to the…rolling around in bed."

She flashed him an irritated glance, but when she saw his smile, she broke into a grin, as well.

"Do you really want to do this?" he asked her.

"Yes. I'll go—if you promise not to push me." She glanced up at him through thick lashes, her gaze flickering down over his chest and abdomen and sighed. "You're very hard to resist."

He leaned back, his arms bracing him on the mattress.

Patience was what was called for with Mari, but he'd never had to tamp down his lust more than this. Maybe he was as aware as she seemed to be that when they made love, no barriers could exist between them. He supposed Mari was saying that some of those obstacles existed for a reason—they were a defense against hurt, against bad judgment.

She had to let down those barriers at her own pace, not his. He wasn't planning on hurting Mari, of course. Look at what'd happened today at his mom's house, though. Marc hadn't wanted that. Pain seemed to be inherent to any scenario that involved Mari and him together.

He was willing to deal with that potential pain, but Mari had to decide on her own if she was willing to endure the bad that might come with the good.

"I guess there are worse things than you finding me irresistible," he murmured ruefully.

She ducked her head, hiding her smile. "Much. But for now..." She nodded significantly toward the window. "Don't break your neck on the way down, Tarzan."

Marc grimaced as he stood and headed toward the window. He was still hard with arousal. "A broken bone might get my mind off some other aches," he said under his breath.

"What?"

"Nothing," he said as he threw one leg out the window and paused, straddling the low sill, his head still inside Mari's room. She watched him with a small smile, her arms crossed beneath her breasts.

"You're sure you want me to go?"

"Quite sure."

"Do you want me to help you out with anything tomorrow?"

She considered for a moment, her mouth pursed. "You could babysit Jenny and Brendan for Colleen. That way we could go over her contract, and I could show her around the facility after she gets off work."

Her eyebrows arched when he frowned. She obviously guessed that he'd have preferred to help out with something a little more hands-on in Mari's company.

"Okay, I'll take Jenny and Brendan to the beach," he conceded. His gaze sharpened on her. "But come Friday morning, we're leaving Harbor Town and everything in it behind for a few days, agreed?"

"Agreed," Mari said.

Marc hesitated when he saw her expression. "Come here," he said after a moment.

She approached the window slowly. When he palmed her jaw he saw tears swell in her eyes.

"What's wrong?" he whispered. "Why do you look so serious?"

"I just don't want to screw up things any further than they already are."

He placed a hand on her hip and leaned forward, pressing a kiss just below her ribs.

"I know you've felt lonely for a long time now," he told her. "But you're not going to be standing alone this time. I promise."

He placed another kiss on her upper abdomen and felt a shudder go through her. He kept his face pressed just below the fullness of her breasts for a few seconds. She smelled so good he needed to concentrate all of his will in order to leave. After a moment, he lifted his head and looked up at her face. She watched him with liquid, fathomless eyes.

"Okay?" he whispered.

She nodded. He leaned forward and kissed her once more—this time on the naked skin above her left breast—and ducked out of the window.

Chapter Ten

Mari arrived at the facility the following afternoon and exclaimed in pleasure when she saw all the bushes and flowers that had been planted. As she alighted from the car, Mari caught a glimpse of her brother carrying a shovel and walking toward the back of the building. Eric Reyes, on the other hand, was crouching and maneuvering a lilac bush into the newly dug earth. He stood as she approached and waved.

"It looks fantastic," Mari enthused. "I can't believe how much you and Ryan have done."

"It's coming along," Eric agreed as he removed a pair of gloves. They were practically the only things he was wearing, besides a pair of shorts, socks and tennis shoes. The sun had deepened his muscular torso to a dark bronze. Mari glanced around when she heard the sound of another car pulling into the lot. Eric's expression stiffened when he saw Colleen step out of the car and start toward them. Mari knew the second Colleen recognized Eric because she halted momentarily and kicked up a few pieces of gravel before she resumed walking.

Mari cleared her throat, acutely aware of the tension in the air as Colleen joined them.

"You two are going to be working together in the future. I'm hoping you'll end up respecting each other as much as I respect both of you," Mari said after she'd greeted Colleen.

She glanced at Colleen, whose chin was slightly raised as she regarded Eric. His expression was also rigid.

Suddenly he smiled, his white teeth flashing in his tanned face. "It's not going to be me starting any fights," he said significantly. "Welcome to The Family Center, Colleen. From what Mari tells me, we're lucky to get you."

Colleen looked a little taken aback, as if she was deciding which parts of Eric's greeting were sarcastic and which parts genuine. "Thank you," she murmured.

Mari sighed and led Colleen into the building to show her around, hoping fervently she hadn't made a mistake by involving both of them. But the fact was, she trusted Colleen and Eric implicitly. It was their working *together* that created some cause for concern.

After they'd toured the facility and Colleen had chosen an office, they sat down together to go over the employment contract.

"Mari... I'll have to tell my mom about the job soon," Colleen said when they were wrapping things up an hour later. "From some of the things you've said so far, I've gotten the impression you were trying to keep the Center under wraps for the time being. Is it okay with you that Mom knows?"

Mari paused in the action of putting a stack of papers

into her briefcase. "Of course you should tell her," she said firmly, although it was trepidation that filled her, not confidence. "She'll have to find out sometime, right? It's inevitable."

"I thought…perhaps *you'd* like to tell her," Colleen said cautiously.

"*Me?* I don't think that's a very good idea. You saw yesterday how your mom feels about me." She sighed when she saw Colleen's worried expression. "Look, I'd like to think that the news about The Family Center will be welcome to Brigit, but I have a feeling she might view it as an insult."

"An insult?" Colleen asked.

Mari nodded. "I hope she doesn't, of course. But that's been haunting me, that your mother might see me starting this project as a sort of sanctimonious slap to the face. It's her town, after all. She might consider it intrusive, as if I'm purposefully throwing the crash into the spotlight again…re-opening old wounds."

"But you're trying to *heal* old wounds. This project is about the future, not the past," Colleen exclaimed.

"I'm so glad you see it that way. But you must see what I mean. Not everyone will agree."

"Like your brother?"

Mari sighed. "Yeah. Like Ryan. He also believes the past should remain safely buried and contained."

Colleen inhaled deeply. "Well, we'll just have to take it one day at a time. People have their opinions, it's human nature. Just because everyone in Harbor Town isn't on board initially doesn't mean we can't change their mind. They'll come around once they see the positive things that come out of The Family Center. The proof is in the pudding, right?"

Mari chuckled, feeling a little less weary. "Bless you, Colleen."

A few minutes later, Colleen checked her watch and gasped. "Look at the time. I'd better get back to make the kids something, or Uncle Marc will have already fed them pizza and Cheetos or something."

"He's not that bad, is he?" Mari asked, grinning.

"No, in all fairness, he's not. Marc would probably throw in an apple and make them drink milk, along with their Cheetos. Liam, on the other hand, thinks pizza ought to be served for breakfast, lunch and dinner, and Brendan totally agrees." Colleen paused in the process of getting her keys out of her purse and glanced at Mari speculatively. "Marc told me you were going with him to Chicago this weekend."

"He did?" Mari asked weakly.

Colleen's aquamarine eyes sparkled. "Yeah. And I think it's a brilliant idea."

"Really?"

"Do you know how rare it is to be given a second chance with someone?" Colleen asked, suddenly sober.

"Colleen, I've meant to say... I'm so sorry about your husband. I wanted to tell you yesterday, but I just never got around—"

Mari was reminded of Colleen's courage when she smiled and stood. "There's no need to apologize, Mari. Darin and I had some wonderful years together. I cherish every moment I had with him. You and Marc should do the same."

"It's hard," Mari admitted. "The future can be so uncertain."

"All the more reason to grab your chance at happiness while you can. I'll talk to you soon," Colleen said before she left the room.

After Colleen was gone, Mari lingered, thinking

about what she'd said. If she looked at it from Colleen's point of view, everything seemed so certain, so clear.

But it wasn't all that cut-and-dried, was it?

Marc had recently been through a divorce. He'd said that a serious relationship or marriage was the farthest thing from his mind. The pregnancy had come from a wild, impulsive moment. What if he wasn't pleased by the news? It was one thing for him to say he wanted to be with her, even when he'd formerly planned to be cautious in the dating arena, but suddenly being strapped with a relationship and a baby was another thing altogether.

Mari locked up the offices, but her thoughtful mood made her stroll toward the woods and the dunes instead of immediately getting in her car. She walked the length of Silver Dune and paused, staring out at the vast, blue lake. The wind whipped her hair around her face. She pictured standing next to Marc on that ledge fifteen years ago.

Stop thinking so much, Mari. Just jump.

Mari wished it was all that simple.

She kept herself busy that night and the following day. Distracting herself with plans and projects for the Center helped her from ruminating on her worries about Marc, the baby, Brigit, Ryan and a dozen other things.

By the time twilight fell on Thursday evening, Mari knew she was going to have to confront Ryan about her plans to go away with Marc the next day. She broke the news while they were cleaning up in the kitchen after dinner.

"A weekend in Chicago?" he asked slowly. "That sounds serious."

"It is, I think," Mari admitted.

"How serious?" Ryan asked, his dark brows drawn together in concern and growing anger.

"Ryan, you're going to have to trust me on this."

"I *do* trust you. I don't trust Kavanaugh. Can't you see the end result isn't going to be good?" he demanded. "There's too much garbage in your pasts, Mari. You deserve something better than that."

"I want to do this. I *need* to do this."

Ryan straightened abruptly from where he'd been leaning on the counter. "His father murdered Mom and Dad. How can you even consider a future with Marc Kavanaugh?"

"It wasn't murder," Mari countered, just as heatedly. "It was an accident!"

"It was reckless *homicide*," Ryan boomed.

For a few seconds, Mari just stood there as her brother's retort echoed in her ears.

"How long?" she asked eventually. When Ryan just pinned her with a furious stare, Mari persisted in a low, trembling voice. "How long are you going to hold on to your anger, Ryan? Mom and Dad are gone. Your anger isn't going to bring them back."

"At least I'm respecting their memory," Ryan said stiffly before he tossed the dish towel on the counter, "which is a damn sight more than you're doing by climbing into bed with Marc Kavanaugh."

Mari didn't get much rest that night. She'd only been asleep for a few hours when she was awakened by the sound of her bedroom window scraping open. A scream building in her throat, she sat up in bed.

"Shhh, it's me."

"Marc Kavanaugh," she scolded in a low, vibrating voice, "I'm going to chop down that elm tree. You scared the daylights out of me. What do you think you're doing?"

"It's Friday morning," he said in a hushed tone. In the

darkness, she saw the shadow of his tall body squeezing agilely through the window.

"It's not even dawn yet," she hissed.

"It's going to be soon. We have to hurry. Come on, get up."

Mari barely suppressed a squawk when he came over to the bed and pulled the sheet off her.

"Have you packed already?"

"Yes, but—"

"Great. I'll take your stuff out to the car while you shower."

Mari blinked when he turned on the bedside lamp. Her mouth was open to protest. But when she saw him— wearing a pair of jeans and a light gray collarless shirt, his hair adorably mussed on his forehead from his tree climbing—he looked so excited and so damn appealing, her irritation faded into mist.

She got out of bed, scowling. She didn't want him to know how attractive she found him at that moment. He already had more power over her than she preferred. "Okay, but this better be worth it. I just got to sleep a couple of hours ago."

"I'll make it up to you. I promise," he said. Pointedly urging her toward the shower, he nodded at the door.

She thought for sure Marc was going to spirit her away to Chicago the second they were both in his car. He surprised her by heading first to The Tap and Grill and returning with a coffee for each of them before turning toward Main Street Harbor.

"Where are we going?" she whispered when Marc told her to leave her purse in the car. Dawn hadn't broken yet. The quiet night and her unexpected awakening had created a hushed, tense feeling of expectation inside her.

"Colleen's boat," he said as they hurried down a long dock, Mari's hand in his. "It used to be Darin's."

"What…? We're going to cross Lake Michigan to get to Chicago?"

Marc's derisive snort was her only answer. Once they reached a moored speedboat, Mari didn't argue when Marc told her to sit down and relax. It would be another hot summer day once the sun rose, but the pre-dawn air was mild and pleasant. A light breeze tickled her cheek as she listened to Marc untie the craft and start the boat.

Within a matter of a few minutes, they'd passed the buoys designating the harbor, and Marc released the throttle. Her curiosity would have to wait. He'd never hear her questions over the roar of the engine. Mari watched the lights of Harbor Town slowly slide to the right of her vision as the boat cut through the water.

Mari studied Marc's silhouette in the darkness when the boat slowed. He was sitting on the back of the seat instead of in it. She realized he was searching for some landmark on the shore.

He abruptly cut the motor, and only the sound of gentle waves slapping against the side of the boat entered her ears.

"This is it," Marc said.

"This is *what?*"

"Come here."

She stood and grasped his outstretched hand. He guided her to the seat in front of him. From that position, Marc was directly behind her, his legs bent on either side of her. He placed one hand on her shoulder and the other along her cheek. He applied a slight pressure until Mari turned her head toward shore.

"Right about there," Marc murmured from above her. The sun had started to rise. Mari could make out the huge shadow of a dune in the distance. She glanced to the right, gauging the distance to Harbor Town.

"It's Silver Dune," she whispered.

"Yeah," Marc replied.

A warm wind whisked past them. Mari shivered, not from the breeze, but from the feeling of Marc's left hand moving along her neck. She went still when he caressed her jaw with his fingertips. When she realized how concentrated her awareness was on the sensation of him close behind her, his legs surrounding her, his stroking hand, Mari rolled her eyes in the darkness. You'd think she was a sixteen-year-old on her first date.

"So what are we doing?" she whispered.

"Watching the sun rise over Silver Dune."

"Why?"

He pressed back on her shoulder, and her head fell in the juncture of his spread legs. Her eyes sprung wide. The location where she her head rested wasn't really decent, but Marc sounded casual enough when he spoke.

"Why not?"

Mari tried to attend to the sunrise, but it was difficult to do, surrounded by Marc's scent and heat. The waves gently rocked them, and Marc stroked her neck and shoulder in the most distracting manner. Slowly, the sky behind the black dune began to turn silver and then to muted gold tinted with rose. Neither of them spoke as they watched the crimson orb of the sun top the horizon and then creep through the woods beyond the sand dune. The trees seemed ablaze. Mari saw a structure in the far distance through the trees and gasped.

"What?" Marc asked gruffly from behind her. His voice sounded close, like he'd leaned close.

Mari twisted her head to try and see him. He groaned, and she realized why. When she hastily tried to lift her head from between his thighs, he rested his hands on her shoulders and kept her in place.

"I can see The Family Center," Mari said quietly.

"I know. I can, too."

The sun topped the tall trees at the top of the dunes and sent its warming rays onto a pale blue, shimmering lake.

"Everyone comes to Harbor Town for the sunsets," Mari murmured after a moment. "But the sunrises are just as beautiful."

"I wanted you to see one."

Mari glanced over at the small town perched on the shore. It looked perfect and fresh, cast in the golden light of dawn. She set down her coffee cup and turned in the seat. When Marc saw what she was doing, he steadied her while she rose to her knees in front of him. His small grin faded the instant before she pressed her mouth to his.

When she leaned back a moment later, and Marc stared down at her, she saw the sunrise reflecting in his blue eyes like glowing embers.

"I know what you wanted me to see," she whispered.

"Do you?"

She nodded and pressed her lips fleetingly to his once again. "You wanted me to see things in a whole new light." She inspected him somberly. "I'm trying, Marc."

He opened his hand along her neck and stroked the line of her jaw with his thumb. "That's all I ask," he said. He nodded toward the shore. When Mari turned, he put his arms around her shoulders and pulled her back against him. "Don't you think that'd be a perfect spot for a memorial?"

"A memorial?" Mari murmured, her cheek pressed against his chest.

"Yeah. A memorial for the survivors of substance abuse. A fountain, maybe, set there at the edge of the trees on the promontory of the dune?"

"It would be. It'd be like a sanctuary, a place to think or pray…"

A place to heal, Mari added in her mind.

"I want to sponsor it," he murmured.

She twisted around and gazed up at him. "You don't have to—"

"I know that," he interrupted. "You don't *have* to do what you're doing, either. Not that this compares to what you're doing, not in the slightest. But it's something I'd like to do, if you'd let me."

"Of course. It's a beautiful idea." She put her arms around his waist and he embraced her in return.

For a few minutes, they bobbed on the blue lake and held each other fast, drinking in the rays of the new day. After a while, he leaned back slightly and put his hand beneath her chin. He tilted her face up and kissed her, chastely at first, but then, as their tastes mingled, with all the focused, fierce passion she associated exclusively with Marc.

"We'd better get going," he said next to her lips a while later.

Looking into his gleaming eyes, she nodded. She took her own seat as Marc started up the boat again.

They returned to the same town she'd known and remembered, but thanks to Marc, Harbor Town looked a little different now in her eyes.

Due to her sleeplessness last night, Mari found herself drifting off when they were only fifteen minutes away from Chicago. When she awoke, they were driving down

Lake Shore Drive with the city to the left and the deep blue lake shimmering to the right of them. She was still blinking into wakefulness when Marc turned off onto Randolph Street. He'd only driven west a half block before he pulled into the parking garage of a high-rise.

"You ready?" Marc asked her a few seconds later, after he'd parked.

Mari nodded, suddenly feeling a little giddy with the excitement of their weekend getaway. He grabbed their bags and led her to an elevator. They stopped in the luxurious, residential lobby so that Marc could collect his mail.

Mari observed with fascination the way Marc transformed from a sun-tanned, easygoing vacationer to a confident, big-city state's attorney right before her eyes. It wasn't a huge change, granted, and he didn't behave any differently in the slightest. The nod of respect a few residents granted him as he picked up a package from his doorman and the wistful, backward glance one attractive, middle-aged woman cast his way allowed Mari to see this different shade to Marc's complex character.

He introduced her to his doorman, Oscar. Oscar treated Marc with equal parts friendliness and deference and seemed to know all sorts of intimate details about Marc's life.

"I've known Mari since I was eleven years old," Marc admitted to Oscar as Mari and the doorman shook hands.

"Oh, the dirt you must have on him," Oscar said with a wink.

Mari opened her mouth, but Marc hastily grabbed her hand and led her away. The sound of Oscar's laughter echoed behind them.

Marc's condo was large and featured a breathtaking lake view. It was decorated in a sparse, austere fashion that she usually associated with a busy man living alone. In Marc's case, though, it didn't strike her as cold, but as utilitarian and elegant in its simplicity. The only contrast to the strong lines and gray-and-beige decor was a wildflower arrangement that sat on the teak dining room table. Mari walked over to it. The huge display looked brilliant with Lake Michigan as its backdrop.

She smiled as she touched a delicate bloom. "The purple iris and yellow daisy," she murmured in amazement. "They're my favorite flowers. I always loved how the yellow was cheerful and the purple was so pensive. Like sun and shade," she murmured, a smile on her lips.

She glanced down and saw a small card leaning against the vase with the words written on it in black ink, *Welcome Mari.*

"How did you know they were my favorites?" she whispered to Marc, who stood watching her from the head of the table.

"I once saw flowers like that pressed on the inside of one of my mother's flower books," he said. "On the wax covering them, she'd written, Mari's favorites, sun and shade."

"Your mother saved them," she said huskily after a moment, touching a soft bloom.

"Yes."

Once the burn of tears had eased, she glanced at him. "Thank you, Marc."

He shrugged. "My assistant, Adrian, deserves the credit for finding them. I don't know how that woman is able to pull off half the things she does."

She smiled. She knew he was trying to play down the surge of emotion she'd experienced, and she loved him for that.

"Come on. I'll show you your room," he said.

He grabbed her suitcase and showed her into what was obviously a guest bedroom, given the lack of personal items on the dresser and bedside tables. Despite its relative bareness, it was still a well-appointed room featuring a lake view and brilliant sunshine flooding through floor-to-ceiling windows. She caught Marc's eye as he turned from setting her suitcase on a low bench. He raised his brows when he saw her amazed, amused expression.

"You didn't actually expect that I was going to put you in my bedroom, did you?" he asked.

"Honestly? I did," Mari said with a laugh as she began to unzip her suitcase.

"Does that mean you wouldn't have minded?"

Mari blinked at the sound of his low voice. He sounded much closer than he had been just a second ago. She glanced over her shoulder and saw him watching her, the hint of a grin on his mouth.

"I would have minded," she told him with a stern look that was ruined by a smile. She turned back to unzipping her suitcase. "In fact, I appreciate you not pressing me about sharing a bedroom. This room is lovely, thank you."

"I'll just let you unpack then," he murmured.

Mari didn't look up until she sensed his tall figure exiting the doorway. If he only knew how much she wanted to surrender completely to the sensual promise in his hot, blue eyes.

Chapter Eleven

He was sitting on the L-shaped couch in the living room, sorting through a small mountain of mail, when she joined him. Briefs and memos nearly bursting out of the supple leather, a case sat next to him on the cushions. He glanced up at her when she sat in the corner of the couch.

"You must have a million things to catch up on with work after being away for a week," she observed.

He carelessly tossed a thick, white envelope onto the wood and glass coffee table.

"To hell with work." He stood and transferred to the cushion next to Mari. He grabbed her hand. "I'm still on vacation."

She laughed. "You needn't feel like you have to entertain me. You woke me up so early this morning, it's not even lunchtime, yet. Work for a while, if you need to. I can only imagine how demanding your job is."

He squeezed her hand. "If you think I'm going to work when I've finally gotten you all to myself, you're nuts."

She started to protest and noticed the way his eyes were fixed on her mouth. She inhaled and caught the hint of his spicy cologne. Heat slowly expanded in her lower belly, a sensation she seemed to always experience in Marc's presence. She covered the hand that held hers and began to idly stroke his index finger, liking how large and different he felt in comparison to her.

"What are we going to do then?" she asked idly.

When he didn't immediately respond, her gaze flew to meet his. He'd been studying her averted cheek and exposed neck like he'd been considering taking a bite out of her. She tried to ignore the thrill that went through her at the thought.

"How about if we take a walk, have lunch somewhere and come back for a swim. There's a nice pool on the roof deck," he muttered.

Mari couldn't help but notice he seemed much more interested in her lips than the plan he proposed. "Okay."

"Mari?"

"Yes?" she asked breathlessly.

"If you keep doing that to my finger, we're not going anywhere."

Mari froze. She looked at their hands resting on the cushion. He'd covered her left hand, but she'd curled the fingers of her right hand around his index finger and had been stroking him slowly. It had taken Marc's heavy-lidded stare and spoken warning to make her realize how suggestive the caress must have seemed.

She released him and stood abruptly.

"I'll just go change then, for our walk." She didn't wait for him to respond before she hurried out of the room.

Mari hadn't been to Chicago for any extended stays since she was a child. She'd come for performances with the orchestra on several occasions, of course, but was usually too tired from traveling, practices and the performance to see much of anything but the interior of Orchestra Hall and her hotel room. She'd forgotten what a lovely city it was sitting next to the topaz jewel of Lake Michigan. Its towering, glittering high-rises and big-city sophistication blended seamlessly with the Midwestern friendliness of its residents.

They walked north along the lakefront among bikers, skaters, joggers and beach-goers. Such a vast sampling of humanity rolled by Mari's view that she challenged herself to be objective in her assessment of the man who walked next to her in comparison. That jogger, for instance, had Marc's height and lean, muscular build, but he didn't move with the confident, easy grace of a born athlete like Marc did. A dark-haired man with an intense, handsome face held his girlfriend's hand as they walked in the other direction, but he didn't look down at his companion with a hot gaze that could make a woman feel like she was the only female on the planet.

"What?" Marc asked when he caught her trying to covertly study him.

"Nothing," Mari said. She tried to hide her smile.

He started laughing at her mysteriousness, and she joined him.

She was being a fool, and she knew it. Wasn't that what they said love did to you?

They walked all the way to Lincoln Park on the lakefront and ate lunch at a little bistro in the park. Afterward, they wandered around the Lincoln Park Zoo without any serious intent and paused at whatever caught their eye. Marc bought her a lemonade, and Mari happily sipped it while she watched from a below-water-level window as a playful polar bear swam back and forth.

"They say humans project all sorts of things onto animals, but I would swear that bear is flirting with you," Marc mused.

Showing off his sidestroke in front of the viewing window, the frisky polar bear plunged in the other direction in the water. It did appear as if he was staring directly at Mari.

Mari glanced at Marc, and merriment swelled inside her. "Jealous?" she murmured.

He just muttered under his breath, grabbed her hand and led her away from the adorable, amorous bear.

On the way back to Marc's, they window-shopped in boutiques on Rush and Oak Street. When Mari saw a swim-and-dive shop, she asked Marc if they could go inside.

"Didn't you bring along the gold swimming suit?" Marc asked when he saw her holding up a sleek maillot.

"Yes," Mari murmured distractedly. "But I'd feel like an idiot wearing that thing in public."

She glanced up when he made a disgusted sound. "You're not going to buy a *one-piece,* are you?" he asked, sounding like she was considering the ultimate sellout.

She just gave him a condemning glance and kept browsing. She lost track of what he was doing, but he reappeared by her side a few minutes later.

"Here. How about this one. It's not quite so skimpy, but it's sexy as hell, like something a James Bond woman would wear," he growled near her ear.

Mari glanced over and saw him dangling a white bikini on his index finger. An innocent smile crossed his face.

"It'll look great with your tan," he coaxed.

"All right. You have good taste," Mari conceded after a moment. The suit really was cute and had a good deal more coverage than Deidre's bikini. She reached for it, but Marc yanked it away.

"I'll get it for you. What?" he asked when she protested. "It's the only time a woman has ever told me I had good taste in clothing. I want to be able to brag about it every time I see you in it."

A few minutes later they exited the air-conditioned boutique and stepped into the sweltering heat of the midday sun.

"Let's catch a cab home," Marc suggested, already stepping to the curb in search of a taxi. They were back inside his pleasantly cool condominium within fifteen minutes.

"Do you want anything to drink before we go up to the pool?" Marc offered as he headed directly to the kitchen.

"No, thanks. I'm going to change."

Marc had more than good taste when it came to swimsuits. He knew her coloring and figure to a T. The suit not only fit her perfectly, but it played up all her assets without seeming indecent. The halter-style bra had sufficient padding in it to make her feel covered but still managed to shape her breasts in a flattering manner, creating a sexy, but tasteful, décolletage. The bottoms were very abbreviated boy shorts that hugged her hips and rode low on her belly. Mari turned back and forth in front of the mirror in the guest bath, inspecting her stomach critically. Was it, indeed, swelling a fraction of an inch farther than its usual limit? She didn't *think* so, but maybe…

"Mari? You almost ready?" Marc called down the hallway.

Mari started, her hand perched just below the slight convexity of her belly. It all hit her in a rush again; that was *Marc Kavanaugh* calling for her to join him.

She was cradling the tiny beginnings of their baby in her palm.

"I'll be right out," she shouted.

She scurried into her sundress and studied her face in the bathroom mirror. When Dr. Hardy had consulted with her, she'd mentioned that many women chose to wait to tell family members, friends and acquaintances about their pregnancies until after the eighth week. Miscarriages could occur, and if everyone already knew about the pregnancy, it made it all that much more difficult to have to break the news at every turn.

Most couples were cautious, even when they might be married and have loving, supportive families. She was willing to bet that the majority of the couples Dr. Hardy talked about were married and didn't live thousands of miles apart. Most of those couples didn't have the emotional baggage and charged history she and Marc shared.

Surely she wouldn't be doing too much harm by keeping quiet about the pregnancy for the time being. *Surely* she'd be doing Marc a huge favor by sparing him this news for a short while? He'd feel obligated to make major, life-altering changes, and what if those changes weren't even warranted, in the end?

Mari honestly couldn't decide if she was being selfish by harboring that thought, or if she was being caring toward Marc by shielding him for the moment. She could see the argument both ways.

Nothing had seemed certain to her since she'd seen Marc in the lobby of the Palmer House. It seemed as if the ground beneath her feet had become prone to frequent earthquakes, and her typical confident stance had turned wary with every new step.

She entered the living room and saw Marc standing near the door wearing board shorts and a turquoise T-shirt. His briefcase was on his shoulder, and he had several towels tucked beneath his arm. As usual, his gaze struck her like a sensual caress.

Marc's desire was the one thing she could count on with the certainty of the rising sun. But was that enough to cushion them for what would undoubtedly be the rough ride of the future?

Marc was glad to see they were the only residents on the pool deck besides an older woman who was doing laps. Hopefully the lady wouldn't linger once she'd completed her exercise, and he'd have Mari all to himself. He set his briefcase on a table shaded by an umbrella and joined Mari by a couple of recliners in the full sun.

"It's beautiful up here," she murmured, walking over to the view that featured Lake Michigan to the east and the skyscraper-packed shoreline to the north and south. She turned and smiled at him as he removed his T-shirt. "I can't believe we're nearly the only ones up here."

Marc shrugged and sprawled on the deck chair. "It's like anything else. People tend to ignore luxuries after a while," he murmured distractedly, most of his attention focused on Mari's fingers as she unbuttoned her sundress. "I've only been up here a couple times this summer myself. *Holy...* I'm a genius."

He raised his sunglasses. Mari paused in the action of tossing her sundress on a chair. Marc was too busy checking her out in her new bikini to really take in the amused expression on her face. Maybe the new suit did have more coverage, but it did amazing things to Mari's figure.

"I'm never going to hear the end of it, am I?" she said under her breath as she came down next to him on a recliner.

"Never," he agreed. "A man has to take credit where credit is due, and I definitely deserve huge accolades for finding that suit." He unglued his eyes from the swells of her breasts in the V of the top and lazily trailed his gaze down her belly and curving hips. Her smooth, golden skin looked downright edible next to the white fabric.

"Marc."

He blinked and glanced up from her lap to her face. She was staring incredulously at him.

"What?"

"We're not alone," she whispered.

"All I was doing was looking," he said, flipping his sunglasses back into place.

"Somehow it didn't seem that innocent," he heard Mari say under her breath.

He chuckled and stood. "Want to get in?" he asked.

"I'll wait. I think it's you who needs to cool off," she said wryly as she dug around in a canvas bag and retrieved a magazine.

He laughed, tossed off his glasses and dove into the deep end of the pool. The water was refreshing, but nowhere near as cold as he needed it to be. After he'd swum some laps, he raised his head. A quick survey of the pool told him Mari and he were alone.

He swam to the side and poked his head up over the ledge. Mari was watching him over the top of a magazine with a smirk on her face. He crooked a finger at her in a come-here gesture. She shook her head, her gaze returning to the page. He continued to beckon her silently, however. She finally stood and sauntered toward him. Instead of sitting on the ledge and easing down into the water next to him, giving him the opportunity to touch her honey-colored, smooth skin, she dove straight over his head into the water. He grinned as he watched her swim underwater toward the shallow end of the pool. He plunged after her. When she reached the end of the pool, he was there a split second before her. He leaned his back against the wall, his feet on the bottom of the pool and his legs bent, like he was sitting on an invisible chair. He grasped Mari's shoulders.

"What are you... How did you get there so fast?" she sputtered as her head came out of the water.

"I was inspired," he told her as he pulled her over a few inches so that she was above him. As her buoyant body drifted down to touch bottom, she encountered him instead. She scooped up some water and splashed him in the face.

"Hey," he murmured, not at all bothered. He wiped the water out of his face while Mari pushed her long, wet hair away from her eyes. There was laughter in her whiskey-colored eyes when they met his.

"I'll race you to the other end," she challenged breathlessly.

"Uh-uh," he said quietly as he arranged her so that she straddled his belly in the water, his weight bracing her. Grasping her upper arms, he brought her closer with his hands until her heaving breasts tickled his chest. It felt good—really good—to have Mari's naked skin sliding ever-so-subtly against his in the cool water. "I like it too much right here."

"Do you?" she murmured, her mouth hovering just inches from his, her breath striking his lips in warm, fragrant puffs of air. He placed his hands on her hips, loving the way the curve of them fit into his palms.

"I think you know the answer to that." He slid his hands along her water-lubricated skin. He felt her go still as he traced the beguiling swells of her hips and the indentation of her waist and then her heaving ribcage. "Do you recall how you told me not to come on so strong during this visit, Mari?"

"Yes," she replied, her eyes glued to his mouth. She gasped softly when he shifted his hands so that his fore-fingers were just below the fullness of her breasts and his palms cradled her ribcage. He felt her heart beating into his palms, rapid and strong.

"If you kissed me right now," he murmured. "I wouldn't be breaking any rules."

"Well, I'd hate to be the one to turn you to tru-ancy."

He held his breath as she slowly leaned forward. She very carefully kissed the drops of moisture off his lips one by one, and then rose to do the same for his nose. He closed his eyelids when she transferred her atten-tion there, her quick, elusive caresses creating a riot of sensation in his body. By the time she'd dried his whole face with her sweet, seeking lips, he was starting to hurt with desire.

Her mouth settled on his. He could just as easily have single-handedly stopped the rotation of the earth than prevented himself from transferring his hands to her upper arms and sliding her closer to him. He gave him-self twenty seconds to drown in the taste of her, twenty seconds to show her how much he wanted her, twenty seconds to glory in the fact that her hunger seemed every bit a match for his.

She whimpered softly when he sealed their kiss and moved away from her.

"I think I'll do a lap or three dozen," he muttered before he plunged into the water. He tried to banish Mari's dazed expression and flushed cheeks from his mind's eye as he set a hard, brisk pace for himself, but it didn't really work.

Not in the slightest.

Slightly winded from his swim, he finally rose from the pool. Mari glanced up from her magazine. He gave her a reassuring smile when he saw her uncertain look. The last thing he'd meant to do was make her feel guilty. He was the one who'd asked for it, and, given the same circumstances, he'd gladly suffer his momentary discomfort again just to feel her supple body gliding next to his and her lips caressing every inch of his face.

"Do you mind if I look over a couple things in the shade?" he asked, pointing toward his briefcase beneath the umbrella.

"No, of course not," she assured.

He dried off and settled himself for the next forty minutes, going through his phone messages and making a priority list for things that needed to get done in the next few days. He was proud of himself for staying on task with the alluring distraction of Mari reclining just feet away in a sexy bikini.

Everything was going great until she pulled some suntan lotion out of her bag and started smoothing the emollient onto her long legs. Like a bee drawn to honey, he rose slowly from his seat at the shaded table and walked toward her.

"You need any help with that?" he asked as he plopped down into the recliner next to her.

"I think I can manage."

He didn't reply as he watched her work the lotion into her thighs. She glanced over at him as she poured some more into her palm.

"I thought you were working," she said with a touch of asperity.

He studied every detail of her hands smoothing over her belly.

"I was. I'm not anymore. You have beautiful arms," he said distractedly.

Mari snorted. "Thanks. I don't think I've ever received that particular compliment before."

He smiled and just continued to watch her. He might have looked relaxed to a casual observer, but in fact, his body was tensed like an animal's ready to spring. Why wouldn't anyone tell her she had gorgeous arms? They were like sensual poetry, the way they gleamed in the summer sun, the way she moved them. Why hadn't he told her before?

He sat up when she reached her shoulders.

"Here," he said, reaching for the bottle. "You're going to get it on your new suit."

She glanced at him doubtfully but released the lotion, nevertheless.

"Lean back," he encouraged as he transferred positions so that he was sitting beside her on her recliner. "It's best to be in the exact spot where you're going to lay when you put the stuff on, or else you take the risk of missing the exposed parts."

"You sound like quite the expert on suntan lotion application," Mari said sarcastically as she reclined in the chair.

Marc poured some of the warm liquid in his palm. "Well, I don't want to brag or anything…"

Mari rolled her eyes, but he sensed her focused attention as he carefully began to rub the emollient onto her shoulder, careful not to stain the fabric of her suit.

"You really take this seriously. You'd think you were doing surgery," Mari murmured as she watched him work the lotion into her skin along the line of the suit.

"I'm a perfectionist," he said in a deadpan tone.

She laughed. The smile remained on her mouth while he did her other shoulder. It faded when he squeezed more lotion in one hand and started matter-of-factly working it into the exposed skin in the V of her halter top. From the periphery of his vision, he saw her mouth open to protest, but he just continued rubbing the lotion over the top of a breast with two fingers, sliding and circling over firm, curving flesh. He leaned down farther, taking his time and true to his word, completing the task with meticulous attention to detail.

It was with great disappointment that he finished covering the last, tiny patch of satiny-smooth skin between her breasts at the very bottom of the V. He straightened and screwed the cap on the bottle.

"There. Not a drop on your new suit," he said as he handed the lotion back to her.

He paused when he finally glanced up into Mari's face. Her cheeks had turned pink. Her lips were parted as she panted shallowly.

He'd been so absorbed in the erotic task of putting lotion on the upper and inner swells of Mari's breasts he hadn't really noticed the effect he was having on her. He opened his mouth to apologize, but wouldn't that be a bit disingenuous? Was he *really* sorry?

"I think I'll go take another swim."

She didn't reply as she watched him stand. He hoped she wasn't angry at him, but Christ... How much temptation could a man take?

You're making a lot of selfish excuses, he remonstrated with himself as he sliced through the water. Mari meant a lot more to him than sex. A hell of a lot more. She'd made a point of saying she wanted to see if there was a chance for them beyond their obvious sexual chemistry. She'd said she didn't want to be pushed. And look at how he was behaving. He couldn't help but recall that both Mari and his mother had made a point of saying he always got what he wanted. Was this the kind of thing they were referring to? He wanted Mari—a hell of a lot—and he couldn't seem to stop himself from touching her, no matter what the circumstances.

The thought sobered him.

He did a racer's flip and soared in the opposite direction.

Problem was, his sexual attraction for Mari was all tied up with a ton of other feelings. It was as easy to turn off his physical desire for her as it was to disengage from his emotional attachment.

But he was going to have to try, if this was going to work. He was going to have to try *harder*. He'd never forgive himself if he got to the end of this weekend and had to live with himself for blowing things with the only woman in the world who mattered.

Mari was feeling exceptionally sleepy by the time they packed up their things and headed back down the elevator to Marc's condominium. Maybe it was the heat, or maybe it was because she'd slept only a few hours last night.

Or maybe it was the fact that she was pregnant.

Whatever the case, Marc took one look at her once they'd walked into his cool, quiet living room and suggested she go take a nap. She was so pleasantly groggy that she didn't argue, but wandered back to the guest bedroom, shut the door and fell asleep almost instantly on the bed.

She awoke later, turned over and saw muted evening light seeping around the blinds.

Thank goodness. She hadn't slept for too long. It would have made her sad to think she'd wasted this rare opportunity with Marc by sleeping away a good chunk of time.

She sprung out of bed, completely refreshed.

Pregnancy seemed to have the effect of making her feel either as wrung out as a limp dishrag or energized, as if she could take on the world...maybe even Marc Kavanaugh.

While she showered, she recalled in vivid detail laying there on that deck chair and watching the intent focus on Marc's face while he slowly, carefully drew little gliding circles over the tops of her breasts. Heat rushed through her body and she turned down the hot water a tad. Mari wasn't sure if it was just Marc's effortless sexuality or the fact that her own body was extra sensitive—perhaps because of the pregnancy—but she'd never known she possessed quite so many erogenous zones.

After her shower, she took time and care with her appearance, wanting to look her best. She styled her hair and applied her make-up sparingly—she didn't need much, thanks to her good color from spending the afternoon in the sun. She dressed in a sleeveless, coral chiffon dress she favored because it worked for everything from a casual evening at home to dinner or cocktails out. The chiffon fabric twisted just beneath the V-neck and followed the same tan line as the suit she'd worn today. Her eyebrows went up when she inspected herself in the dress. Maybe her stomach wasn't starting to protrude, but her breasts definitely looked fuller than usual beneath the soft fabric.

She finished off the outfit with gold hoop earrings, a wrist cuff, sandals and then completed her preparation with a spritz of her favorite perfume. Her heart sank a little in disappointment when she entered the large living/dining room area and didn't see Marc anywhere. Had he thought she was going to sleep through the night, and left to run some errands? No—it looked as if he'd set the dining room table for two. In the distance, she heard a shower running in the master bath.

She smiled as she perused his bookcases in the living room. She was glad they were staying in for the evening.

One could always learn so much about a person from their books. Marc's shelves were filled with everything from autobiographies and biographies to historical books and popular thrillers. She pulled out one of three unlabeled black books and murmured happily when she realized it was a photo album of Marc's younger years.

She sat in the corner of the couch and began leafing through the album. Derry Kavanaugh's face leaped out at her from one photo. It was a rare family shot of the whole Kavanaugh family on one of the Harbor Town white beaches. One single moment of happiness had been captured for eternity, Mari thought as she brushed a finger across Marc's adolescent face. Derry's hair was a mixture of gold and gray, and his handsome, smiling face made him look as if he didn't know the meaning of sorrow. The photo had caught Brigit Kavanaugh staring at her husband, love softening her features.

She felt a bond with Brigit in that moment. They were both grown women who had fallen in love with charismatic Kavanaugh men. They had both lost those men in different ways.

If Brigit had a second chance with Derry Kavanaugh, would she take it? She took another look at a Brigit's loving expression as she stared at her husband and had her answer.

Her heart felt a little heavy or full—Mari couldn't decide which—when she turned the page. For a few seconds, she just stared. After a moment, she carefully picked up the wax-paper envelope with the two flowers that had been dried and preserved—the daisy and the iris. She saw the words Marc had quoted back to her written in Brigit's slanted, clear hand—*Mari's favorites. Sun and shade.* The envelope had been placed beneath a photo of her and Marc standing in the Kavanaugh backyard, Marc's arm around her, both of them grinning broadly, sunburned and flushed with first love. She must have been about sixteen, Marc nineteen.

"I took it when I found it at Mom's."

Mari glanced up at the sound of Marc's gruff voice. Through the film of tears over her eyes, she saw that his hair was still damp and that he wore a pair of jeans and a casual blue cotton button-down shirt. She must have had a slightly bewildered expression on her face because he seemed to find it necessary to clarify.

"The flowers, I mean. I figured...you know."

"What?" Mari asked when he didn't finish.

"I figured they belonged here with me."

For several seconds, neither of them spoke.

"I didn't really have anything of yours after you left," Marc explained. "Except for photos." He inhaled and glanced out the windows to the lake in the distance. "Truth be told, I sort of stole it from Mom. I didn't want to have to deal with her questions if I asked for permission for them."

"When did you take them?" Mari asked in a hushed voice.

Marc met her gaze again. "One weekend...after the Palmer House."

Mari swallowed and carefully replaced the dried flowers in the book. She stood and slid the photo album back into its place on the shelf. When she turned, she saw him examining her appearance.

"You look gorgeous. You dressed up. I ordered in some food for us, but we can go out if you like."

"No," she said quickly. "I'm glad you planned to stay in."

His grin caused something to hitch in her chest. "I'll take you for dinner tomorrow night. Some place nice. Tonight, I ordered in from a favorite restaurant—French Vietnamese cuisine. They already delivered. It's warming in the oven."

"Great."

"I have some wine chilled," he said, pointing toward the kitchen. "I'll just…"

Mari stepped forward, halting his exit by placing her hand on his arm. He looked down at her, surprised by her abrupt movement. Standing this close, she could smell the scent of his soap and spicy cologne and could see the flecks of green in the midst of the sky-blue of his iris.

"Thank you," she said.

"For what? Stealing some dried flowers?"

"No. For not forgetting me…for not giving up."

She went up on her tiptoes and kissed him fleetingly on the mouth. When she lowered and looked up at him, she saw that he looked stunned.

"How about that food? I'm hungrier than I thought I would be." She tilted her head toward the kitchen in a silent prompt.

He blinked, seeming to come out of his daze. "Right," he said. "Dinner."

Mari smiled as she followed him. He was usually so confident. It did something to her to see him off balance, even if it had lasted for all of two seconds.

Marc had ordered multiple items, so they opened all the cartons and spooned small portions from each onto their plates. The food was some of the best she'd ever eaten, and Mari didn't think it was just because of the company. There was steamed Chilean sea bass with cellophane noodles and oyster mushrooms; jumbo shrimp, asparagus and scallions; diced filet mignon and yams in a light sate sauce and a lovely salad made with lotus root, cucumber, tomatoes and a tamarind dressing.

Just as Mari picked up her fork to begin, Marc hopped up from his seat. "Hold on… I forgot."

He came back into the dining room carrying a candlestick and brand new taper. Grinning, he lit the candle and sat down across from Mari.

"So proud of yourself, aren't you?" she teased as she forked a succulent shrimp.

"Well, you've got to admit, when you get a caveman to serve you fine cuisine by candlelight, it's a small miracle, right?"

Mari gave a small moan as she chewed the shrimp. "You did *very* well, Caveman."

A while later she leaned back in her chair and sighed as she stared out at the dark blue lake and muted lavender sky. The flickering candle was starting to cast shadows on the ceiling. It would be dark soon. She lazily forked her last bite of salad and chewed it slowly, appreciating the subtle blend of flavors on her tongue.

"I think I've died and gone to heaven," she murmured.

"I'm glad you liked it." He nodded at her full wine glass. "Wine not to your liking?"

"Oh… No, it's fine," she said hastily. "The food was so delicious I didn't have a thought for it, that's all."

"You can take it into the living room, if you like," he suggested. "I got dessert, but maybe we should wait a bit?"

"Definitely," Mari agreed.

He stood and began to clear their dishes. When Mari started to help him, he shooed her off, insisting she take her wine and relax in the living room. Mari obligingly took her full glass of wine, but felt a little awkward since she had no intention of drinking it. She kicked off the sandals she was wearing, perched in the corner of the L-shaped couch and drew up her feet. When Marc joined her a few minutes later, he carried a mug and handed it to her.

"Figured you'd probably prefer tea. It's herbal," he said as he handed it to her.

"Thank you," she murmured, scooting her feet back a few inches to make room for him to sit.

"I was just thinking while I was cleaning up in the kitchen—I'm not used to being around you as an adult. I shouldn't have assumed you drink alcohol." He continued when she stared at him in blankly, "I've never seen you drink since I met up with you at the Palmer House. It wouldn't surprise me if you abstained."

"I have a glass of wine once in a while," she said as understanding dawned. He'd assumed she hadn't drank her glass of wine for reasons related to their past. In truth, she hadn't drank it because of her pregnancy. "What I said was true. It just didn't appeal tonight."

Marc nodded, but his expression was somber. "I mentioned it the other night, but I'll say it again. I'm not much of a drinker, either. I just thought some wine with the food—"

"Marc," she interrupted. "I didn't think twice about you having a glass of wine. You didn't even finish it. Do you really think I'm worried that you're some kind of alcoholic because your father had a drinking problem?"

He shrugged and glanced away. "It's not as if I haven't heard something similar before. My brother and sisters have, at one time or another. All of us were stained by my dad's actions."

Mari opened her mouth to demand the details—who

had dared to insinuate something so ridiculous? How could they possibly justify their allegations, when the Kavanaugh children were practically paragons of virtue, dedication and hard work?—but she closed her mouth when she noticed Marc's rigid profile.

"It's so unfair. I'm sorry," she murmured.

His gaze returned to her face. "It meant a lot, to discover you weren't one of those people judging me for someone else's actions," he said quietly.

She shook her head, her throat suddenly tight with emotion. She cradled his jaw with her hand and moved her fingers, absorbing the sensation of his warm skin, both overwhelmed by his vibrant presence and hungry to experience more of him.

"What's wrong?" he asked her as he studied her through narrowed eyelids.

"Life is so uncertain. I wish…I wish I could always have you like this."

"Like this?" His mouth quirked, and Mari brushed her thumb against his lips. He went still at her touch.

"Just us," she whispered as she moved her finger, studying his texture like her thumb was her only source of sensation. "No one else."

"It is just us. And the future," he said.

"There's the past."

His hand came up and cradled her shoulder. "There's the present, Mari."

The present.

Staring into Marc's eyes, she felt the present moment stretching out to eternity. He didn't move or speak when she leaned over and placed her mug of tea on the coffee table, but she sensed the tension that had leaped into his muscles. She lifted her knee and straddled his thighs, her head lowered. The need she felt couldn't be denied any longer.

She unfastened the first three buttons of his shirt and pressed her face into the opening.

She did what she'd been holding back from doing for weeks now...for years.

She drowned herself in him.

Chapter Twelve

The skin on his chest felt thick and warm pressed against her seeking lips. He didn't have an abundant amount of hair there, but what she encountered delighted her as she rubbed her cheek and lips against it, experiencing the springy, soft sensation. His scent filled her, intoxicated her. She moved her hands, cradling his waist and then sliding up the taper to his ribs, caressing him with gentle, molding palms and eager fingers.

It took her a few seconds to realize he was holding his breath. That changed when she gently pulled aside the fabric of his shirt and kissed a dark copper-colored nipple.

He gasped her name raggedly and tangled his fingers in her loose hair.

He was so hard, so male. Her lips and fingertips couldn't seem to get enough of him. She rubbed her mouth across his nipple, testing the texture with her tongue, thrilling to the sensation of the flesh beading beneath her caress. Her hands moved fleetly, unbuttoning the remainder of his shirt. His abdomen and ribs rose and fell as she explored his naked torso and tasted his skin.

He said something in a low, rough tone when she moved her mouth, raining light, quick kisses on his chest. She couldn't hear him, but interpreted the words to mean desire. He hissed her name when she greedily sampled another small, flat nipple and felt it grow stiff below her tongue and lips.

He cursed and grasped her shoulders, lifting her. He pulled her down to him and seized her mouth, and their separate fires leaped into a single inferno.

He joined her in her quest to explore, to touch…to thrill. His hands molded her back muscles and encircled her waist. She loved how big he was, how much of her he could hold in his grasp. He shifted her slightly on top of him, bringing her closer against him, matching the core of her heat to his.

They groaned into each other's mouths, burning separately…burning as one.

Mari felt liberated. Before, she'd allowed herself to touch Marc's fires, to be consumed by them, even. This was the first time she'd let her own flames run free. Before, there had always been the nagging restraint, the hovering caution.

Not now, though. Not in this eternal moment.

He shifted his hands to her hips, his fingers delving into the soft flesh of her buttocks. They continued to devour each other as he rocked her against him, both of them so hungry, so starved for one another. He moved one hand to the back of her head and held her while he ravished her mouth. His lips lowered, feeling hot and voracious on the skin of her neck. She tilted back her chin and arched her back, offering herself to him, lost in a sea of sensation. His hands moved rapidly as he pressed kisses against her neck and shoulders, sweeping aside the fabric of her dress and the straps of her bra. He peeled cloth off her breasts. Mari cried out in abrupt loss when suddenly his mouth was gone, then gasped as his mouth closed over a nipple. She furrowed her fingers through his short hair and held him to her as she whimpered in sublime pleasure. An unbearable ache swelled inside her, a pain she knew would only be silenced by their joining. He continued to tease her flesh with his mouth and tongue until Mari grew desperate. She reached between them, wild to remove the barrier of their clothing. His head rose when he realized what she was doing. His breath came in short, jagged pants against her damp breasts as they fumbled, united in a fury of need.

Her head fell back and she gasped at the sensation of him entering her.

"Look at me."

She complied with his command. It felt as if she'd explode from the strength of her combined emotion and arousal when she met his fierce gaze. She rested in his lap, quivering. She felt so full...so inundated with him.

They began to move at the same moment as if by some unspoken agreement. He closed his eyes. A muscle twitched in his cheek. She understood the sweet agony. She experienced it with him.

"You've been holding yourself back from me," he whispered hoarsely, his eyes open now, pinning her as she moved over him.

She didn't reply. Her body spoke for her. It was true, but she wasn't holding back from him now.

And she made sure he knew it.

She leaned down and scraped her parted lips against his, caressing rather than kissing. She tasted his sweat.

Their breaths mingled and the inferno inside her grew. His hold on her hips and buttocks tightened and they both became more demanding, both of the other and themselves.

She wanted to hold onto these seconds forever…never wanted it to end.

If it didn't end this moment, she would die.

She held on tight to his shoulders and cried out in pleasure as she succumbed. She heard his low, rough growl as he held her down to him, felt his muscles grow rock hard beneath her clutching fingers. Her name was a fierce prayer on his tongue.

The seconds unfolded into minutes as time resumed its normal cadence. Mari pressed her lips against Marc's pulse as she tried to catch her breath. She felt his leaping heart slow to a steady throb.

Something had happened.

She had the amazingly clear thought through her hazy satiation: She *had* to tell Marc about the baby, and not just because she was obligated. In that moment she wanted to tell him, *longed* to complete the link between herself, this vibrant man she held and their growing child with every living cell in her being.

She whimpered in protest when he lifted her, separating them. He groped for his jeans, roughly pulling them up around his hips.

"No. I don't want it to end," she murmured.

"It's not going to end."

She blinked when she heard the hard edge to his voice. Then he was gathering her to him and standing.

The master bedroom was dim and shadowed. The duvet felt cool against her heated skin when he laid her on his bed. He came down over her.

"It's only the beginning," he said in a gruff whisper and his mouth settled on hers.

* * *

Mari quickly learned he was right. They made love again and then held each other.

She considered how she would tell him about the baby. Now, perhaps, when they held each other and their desire for one another still lingered around them like a comforting cocoon? Her heart felt so full at the moment, though. She didn't want to tell him in a rushing torrent of emotion and end up crying on his chest, feeling like a fool.

Perhaps tomorrow while they were out at dinner would be a safer choice, she thought nervously.

"What are you concentrating on so hard?" Marc interrupted her thoughts.

She glanced up at his face, surprised. "Was I?"

He gave her the slow grin that always caused a funny sensation in her belly and brushed a tendril of hair off her brow. "You looked like you were plotting how to break some terrible news. I have a feeling I know what it is."

She sat up slightly, alarmed. "You do?"

He nodded, suddenly sober.

"I made the criminal offense of not giving you your dessert."

Mari rolled her eyes. He laughed and clambered out of bed, telling her to sit still. When he returned, Mari smiled at the vision of him, naked and magnificent and carrying a tray which he set on the bedside table.

"Dessert is served," he told her, coming down next to her on the bed. He flipped the bedside lamp to a dim setting. He turned and dipped a spoon into a small carton and then a dish.

"What's this?" she murmured when he held the spoon to her mouth.

"Fresh pineapple and homemade coconut ice cream."

Mari opened her lips and sweet, rich flavor burst on her tongue.

"Oh…you're going to spoil me," she groaned.

His teeth flashed white against his tan skin when he grinned. He removed the spoon from her mouth, but pressed the cold, smooth metal against her lower lip, massaging the flesh in a small circle.

"That's the plan," he murmured, his tone a gentle, sensual threat.

He gathered more ice cream and fruit and pressed it once again to her mouth. She laughed.

"You don't have to feed me, Marc."

"We should try and get some of it into your stomach."

"So you can get the rest of it in yours?" she joked as the confection melted on her tongue.

"I'll end up eating plenty, don't worry."

He turned from gathering more ice cream on the spoon. Instead of pressing it to her mouth, however, he placed a dollop on the tip of her breast. Mari barely had time to gasp at the unexpected chill when his mouth was there, hot and agitating. Her eyes went wide at the erotic sensation of bitter cold on her nipple transforming so quickly to delicious heat. She grabbed onto his head and sighed. Did he somehow sense how sensitive her breasts were? How much pleasure he gave her with his fingers and mouth? He seemed so focused on them… as if he somehow knew.

Or perhaps it had nothing to do with her body burgeoning with new life. Maybe her flesh would always react this way to Marc's touch?

The idea was a little disorienting.

He drew on her nipple and her thoughts splintered in a thousand directions. Her eyelids flickered closed as she gave into yet another wave of delicious pleasure.

* * *

Drowning.

He felt like he was drowning in her. Marc had told her last night he drank sparingly, if at all, and that had been the truth, but he could easily become addicted to Mari…to the vision of her smile, the way her muscles quivered in anticipation when he kissed the side of her ribs or her belly, the sweet sounds that came from her throat when he was deep, deep inside her.

After a night and most of the following day, Marc started to feel like a heel for keeping her captive in bed for all that time. Not that Mari seemed to mind, but still. It was another gorgeous sunny day, surely they should try and get out and enjoy it some? They were too enraptured with each other to notice much of anything else.

Nevertheless, they showered and ate a late lunch at the café around the corner. Afterward, they went back up to the pool where they were glad to see they were the only ones present. They took a quick swim and returned to their recliners, the hot sun on his skin feeling more like a sensual caress than usual because Mari was lying next to him.

"Marc."

He blinked when she said his name. He hadn't realized he'd been staring at the sight of her belly and hips sparkling with droplets of water.

"Hmm?" he asked.

She shook her head and laughed. "You're a lecher, you know that?"

"If I am, it's with good reason," he muttered as he reached into Mari's bag. "I've waited a hell of a long time." He regretted his words when he saw her expression go solemn. He held up the infamous bottle of suntan lotion from the day before. "Time to oil up."

Her serious look disappeared as she collapsed into giggles. When he started to smooth the lotion onto her soft, warm skin, though, all the tension he'd felt yesterday returned. His smile faded and Mari's laughter quieted.

He managed to cover her upper arm and right shoulder with lotion before their stares met and held. They both stood by silent mutual agreement and grabbed their things. He took her hand and led her back to his condo.

The fact that they'd held themselves on such tight leashes the previous day added to their sense of haste. Perhaps it was half a lifetime spent apart that heightened their sense of need.

Maybe it was the dark worry that these were stolen days with Mari that added to Marc's desperate hunger for her.

"We have to go back to Harbor Town tomorrow," Mari whispered wistfully next to his chest a while later. They lay entangled on his bed, their hearts still thumping rapidly from their latest explosive joining.

He ran his fingers through her long hair and marveled once again at its softness. "That's a long time away still. I'm taking you out to dinner tonight. We have more than twenty-four hours together," he murmured. "That's plenty of time."

"Plenty of time for what?" she asked, pressing her lips to his chest.

"Plenty of time for me to convince you to spend the rest of your life with me."

He'd said it lightly enough, but she must have caught the thread of seriousness in his tone, because she lifted her head. Her eyes looked dark, soft and velvety in the shadowed room.

"How can you be so certain that's what you want?" she whispered.

"You know me. I'm a decisive guy," he said, smiling in order to lighten the moment. He didn't like the anxiety in Mari's eyes.

"But…but you and Sandra divorced only a year and a half ago, and what about—"

"Are you implying it's a complete impossibility?" he asked as he stroked the nape of her neck.

"Well…no."

He met her stare. "There's still time, then." He pressed gently with his fingertips and she put her head back on his chest. "I think there might be time for a little nap, too. You wear me out, Mari."

He smiled when he felt the vibrations of her small chuckle.

She lay awake and watched Marc sleeping, detailing every line of his face. It was true she had an ocean of doubt about their being together, but she had faith in Marc.

She tried to imagine his expression tonight at dinner when she told him about the baby. She drowsily pictured his look of incredulity slowly morphing to one of amazement and excitement.

And love?

Her eyelids opened heavily a while later. The sound of a cell phone ringing insistently had finally penetrated her deep sleep. She lifted her head.

"Marc. That's yours. They've called back several times now, I think. It must be important."

His eyes popped open. He scowled as he rolled over to the far side of the bed and reached for the phone on the bedside table. He glanced at the caller identification before he answered.

"Yeah?" he asked in a deep, sleep-roughened voice.

A long silence ensued. Mari glanced over at him. His profile was rigid with concentration as he listened to the caller. A sense of unease stole over her lassitude.

"How long has it been since she admitted her to the hospital?"

Mari gathered the loose sheet around her and sat up in the bed, her heart starting to hammer rapidly in her chest.

"Uh-huh. Okay. Yeah. We can be in Harbor Town in a few hours. Traffic should be nothing right now...I know, I understand...I still want to come... Yeah, okay. See you soon."

He hit the End button.

"What is it?" Mari asked.

"It's my mom." He met her eyes before he set the cell phone on the table. "She had a heart attack."

"Oh, my God—" Mari whispered.

"It's not bad," he said hastily, hearing her shock. "She's going to be fine. That was Liam calling. It was relatively mild. The cardiologist told Liam and Colleen she's had high blood pressure and high cholesterol for a while now, but according to the doctor, it hasn't improved with treatment. The cardiologist implied my mom hadn't been taking her medications."

"Did you and Liam and Colleen know—"

"No. She never told us. I thought she was completely healthy," Marc interrupted grimly.

"She *looks* so healthy. She's so slender and active. It's the last thing I would have expected."

"Yeah. Me, too," he said in a flat tone.

Mari's chest ached for him. She knew what he was experiencing.

"Anyway...Liam says they'll likely release her tomorrow, but I still want to go."

"Of course," Mari said. She started to rise from bed when Marc put his hand on her forearm, halting her. She looked over at him.

"This doesn't change anything. Do you understand?"

He seemed to regret the harshness of his tone. He closed his eyes and exhaled. "I only meant… I'm sorry, Mari."

"Don't apologize," she said fervently. "I understand completely. Of *course* you have to go. It's family."

He opened his eyes. "Yeah. But I'm sorry nonetheless."

She nodded and hurried out of bed. The vivid dreams about telling Marc about the baby slowly faded to the background.

Chapter Thirteen

They arrived back in Harbor Town that evening at about six. Mari insisted upon accompanying Marc to the hospital.

"I mean... I won't go into your mother's room or anything—that would upset her—but I'd like to be there for you. If you'd like it, anyway."

Marc had given her a half smile and grabbed her hand. "'Course I want you there."

Once they'd located the unit where Brigit was staying, Mari told Marc she was going to find them something to drink while he went and saw his mother. Her throat was dry after the long drive. She left him to confer with the nurse and wandered through the corridors of the hospital in search of a vending machine.

When she returned to the unit carrying two orange juices, she found Marc talking to Colleen in the waiting area. They were the only two occupants in the room, their backs turned to her. Mari went still when she heard the distress in Colleen's tone as she spoke in a quiet, shaking voice to her brother.

"It's my fault," Colleen said.

"What? How could it be your fault? Don't be ridiculous."

"All right, maybe it wasn't entirely my doing, but what I said to her certainly didn't help matters," Colleen said in a hard voice. She swept her long hair over one shoulder in an anxious gesture and leaned back in the chair. "It was after I spoke to her that she got all quiet. Then her complexion went sort of gray and she clutched at herself like this." Colleen demonstrated by grabbing at the area between her left chest and shoulder. "She said she was having a cramp. It scared the hell out of me."

Marc put an arm around his sister for reassurance.

"Yeah, it must have been scary. But it wasn't because of anything you did or said. The doctor said this has been building for a while. Mom hasn't been attending to her treatment."

"What I said didn't help any."

"I doubt that. What were you talking about?" Marc asked, seeming disbelieving and curious all at once.

Feeling guilty for eavesdropping upon the conversation, Mari had stepped forward to identify herself when Colleen spoke in a low, flat tone.

"I told her about my new job. I told her about Mari starting up The Family Center. At first, I thought her silence just signaled her disapproval, but then I noticed her complexion, how odd she looked—"

Marc suddenly looked over his shoulder, his blue eyes pinning her. Had she made a sound? Mari thought perhaps she had.

A sound of distress.

"Mari," Colleen said breathlessly as she stood.

"Mari?" Marc asked, his voice louder than Colleen's had been.

Mari blinked. How long had she been standing there while her heart hammered in her ears? Marc was coming toward her, his brows drawn together. She stupidly offered him a bottle of juice.

"It's not very cold," she said. "I think the vending machine was broken."

He looked at her like she'd been speaking in Swahili. He put his hand on her upper arm. She started. She hated the way his jaw hardened at her instinctive recoil from his touch, but there was nothing Mari could do.

That old feeling of helplessness had risen in her again.

"I think I should go," she said quietly to Marc.

"Because of what you just heard?" Marc demanded, blue eyes flashing.

"Mari, please don't," Colleen said hastily. "I was feeling sorry for myself. I'm sure what I said to Mom had nothing to do with—"

"You don't believe that," Mari interrupted levelly. She turned back to Marc and handed him the other bottle of juice. He seemed so stunned by unfolding events that he accepted it automatically.

"I'll take you home," he said.

"No. I can walk." She didn't know what had come over her, but she felt strangely calm despite her rapid heartbeat. She met Marc's stare, trying her best to seem reassuring even though she felt powerless at that moment. "Everything will be okay, Marc. I'll get my things from you later. You should see your mother right now."

Marc looked like he was about to protest when Colleen spoke, sounding a little weary.

"I'll take Mari home. It'll take me five minutes. You should go on in, Marc. Mom's waiting for you."

Mari didn't glance back when Colleen touched her elbow. They walked away.

When she arrived home, Ryan came down the hallway, bare-chested and holding a butter knife. He wore a pair of cargo shorts and a surprised expression.

"I thought you weren't coming back until tomorrow."

"We came back a little early," Mari said. She parked her rolling suitcase at the bottom of the stairs and placed her fingertips on her eyelids. When she opened them, she was staring at a steely bicep.

"Cool tattoo," she said dully, examining the artist's rendering of the logo of the Air Force wings morphing into an eagle taking flight. "When did you get that?"

"Two...three years— Who cares?" he asked, interrupting himself impatiently. "Are you okay, Mari?"

"Yeah. I'm just really, really tired. I need to go to bed." She started up the stairs, but turned back. Ryan was staring at her with something close to alarm. "I'm okay, Ryan. Marc's mom just had a heart attack. It took us by surprise, that's all."

His mouth dropped open.

"Like I said, I'm just tired. Can you do me a favor?"

"Of course. Anything."

"I don't want any visitors. No one."

Ryan nodded, looking somber.

Mari sighed and trudged up the stairs. She was too fatigued to think...to feel. She felt as if weariness had soaked into her very bones.

This was the ending to their magical weekend. Somehow, it didn't surprise her.

Her bedroom faced west, so it was bright with sunshine. She began to draw the curtains. When she reached the window next to the elm tree, she made sure it was locked before she shut out the remainder of the golden evening light. She thought of how she'd planned to spend that evening in Marc's arms after telling him about her pregnancy.

But the past had a way of sneaking up on you when you least expected it.

The next day Mari stayed to herself. She kept her cell phone turned off. Ryan treated her as if she was recovering from an illness. He seemed like he wanted to question her, but was too sensitive of her mood to interrogate her, for which Mari was thankful. She needed to think.

She was playing her cello at around one o'clock when she paused, hearing tense, male voices downstairs. She held her breath and tried to make out the words.

It was Marc and Ryan. It sounded like they both stood at the front door. Their voices were muffled, but their volume increased with almost every word.

"She doesn't want to see you," Ryan suddenly shouted, plenty clear enough for her to hear.

"Who the hell are you? Her jailer?" Marc responded, just as aggressively.

"I'm doing what she *asked* me to do, Kavanaugh. She *said* she didn't want to see you."

Mari hastily set down her bow and started to rise—she wouldn't be surprised, given the animosity between Marc and Ryan, if a fight broke out—but then the screen door banged loudly and silence ensued.

She set aside her cello and raced over to the window. She opened the sash and searched the leafy branches, dreading seeing Marc's face…and longing for it. The robins remained the only occupants of the elm tree.

A moment later, she sat on the edge of her bed. She realized distantly her cheeks were wet with tears. The memory of studying Marc's face while he slept yesterday afternoon came back to her in graphic detail.

Such a beautiful man.

What parts of Marc would be in their baby? Would their child have his eyes? His sense of humor? His fierce courage?

Thinking about discovering those wonderful characteristics in their child without Marc there to share those moments caused grief and sadness to slice through her like a knife.

She wrapped her arms around her belly as if she was staunching a wound. Tears gushed down her cheeks. She lay on her side on the bed and suffered in solitude.

She awoke the next morning regretting the way she'd been avoiding Marc. He deserved better than to be turned away at her front door like an annoying salesman. She resolved to call him later. She wanted to ask him about Brigit. Marc must be worried sick about his mother. It certainly sounded as if her heart attack hadn't been a major one, but why hadn't she been following her doctor's orders?

She had an appointment at the obstetrician's office that afternoon, and she needed to complete a few more things for The Family Center. Eric, Natalie and she had planned for an opening at the end of August. She regretted nothing more than how Brigit Kavanaugh had responded to the news of the project, but Mari would move forward, nevertheless. Hesitation now twined with her determination to open The Family Center, but the idea of stopping now when their intentions were so good seemed very wrong, indeed.

Her appointment at the obstetrician's went quickly, much to Mari's surprise. The obstetrician, Anita Carol, was a friendly, African-American woman, a few years older than Mari. Mari told her about the bouts of dizziness and nausea, and Dr. Carol recommended frequent, small meals to keep her blood sugar steady and prevent nausea.

She did a quick exam and told Mari make an appointment for an ultrasound. Mari wasn't planning on being in Harbor Town that much longer but she didn't bring that up to the doctor.

"The baby's father can come to the ultrasound, as well," Dr. Carol said brightly on the way out the door. "We should be able to determine the sex by that time, if you two are interested in knowing."

Mari remained seated on the chair in the exam room after the doctor left. She rubbed her belly through her jeans, feeling hollow inside...empty...*lonely* at Anita Carol's parting words.

She irritably wiped at her eyes when they stung. How could she possibly cry more when she'd shed bucketfuls of tears yesterday?

She came to a standstill outside of Dr. Carol's office when she saw Brigit Kavanaugh. Brigit also halted abruptly in the hallway.

"Brigit. Are you...are you well?" Mari asked once her lungs unstuck and she could breathe again. She anxiously searched Brigit's face. She would never have guessed Brigit had been in the hospital the day before yesterday for a heart attack. Dressed in jeans and a fashionably belted turquoise tunic, she looked quite healthy.

For a few tense seconds, Mari wondered if their chance meeting was going to a repeat of the one on Main Street. She exhaled in relief when Brigit spoke, albeit stiffly.

"I'm fine. They released me yesterday morning. The doctor says there was no significant damage to my heart.

I'm just here to fill some prescriptions at the hospital pharmacy."

"Thank God," Mari whispered.

"You were here for an appointment?" Brigit asked, glancing behind Mari.

"Yes," Mari mumbled. Too late, she turned and noticed where Brigit stared. The nameplate on the door read Anita Carol, M.D., Obstetrician. Brigit's glance flickered down over Mari's abdomen. For an awkward moment, neither of them spoke.

"I heard from Colleen about the project you're starting for the survivors of substance abuse."

Mari tried to swallow but her mouth felt too dry. "I... yes. Can we sit down, Brigit?"

Brigit drew herself up tall. "I assure you I'm fine. I feel very healthy. I'm not going to have another heart attack," Brigit said crisply.

Mari smiled. "Actually, I was asking if we could sit down for me."

The straight line of Brigit's frown quivered. "Of course," she said quickly. "Just over here." She led Mari to a bench in the quiet hospital hallway. "Take a deep breath," Brigit said briskly once they sat. "You've gone pale as a ghost."

Mari followed her advice, trying desperately to calm her rioting thoughts. After several seconds of silence, Brigit spoke.

"I don't suppose you could have started this Family Center in San Francisco?"

Mari blinked at the sound of Brigit's wry tone.

"I didn't plan for it in Harbor Town to upset you. I meant for The Family Center to be a positive thing...a healing thing, not a source of upset."

Brigit looked incredulous. Mari sighed heavily, feeling defeated.

"I'm sorry. I can see you feel otherwise," she said quietly. "I can only pray you'll eventually believe me when I say I never meant to cause you any serious harm or pain."

Brigit didn't respond. Perhaps she felt it was unnecessary, given the circumstances.

"I understand you were with Marc in Chicago over the weekend."

Mari levelly met Brigit's stare. "Yes."

"He's determined to have you, no matter what I say. He's always been that way, as you probably recall." The older woman sighed and looked at the opposite wall. She seemed lost in her thoughts. "Once he set his mind to something, Marc always got his way. Even when Derry died, even after all the money for his law school tuition was taken away, Marc just plowed ahead. He went to the University of Michigan instead of Yale where he'd been accepted and planned to go. The tuition was much less expensive, although far from cheap. He worked two jobs and had to take out loans, but he got his degree with honors. Did he tell you that?"

"No," Mari whispered through leaden lips.

"He wouldn't have said anything, I suppose. Not to you." She turned and looked at Mari. "You were the one thing he wanted and couldn't have. It doesn't surprise me, the way he's pursuing you. It's in his character, I suppose."

"You don't admire his determination in this instance," Mari said.

"Determination? I'd call it stubbornness and pride, wouldn't you?" Brigit shifted her purse onto her shoulder and stood. She hesitated. "Take care, Mari. You don't seem entirely yourself."

Mari remained seated as Brigit walked away.

* * *

Her heart felt like a stone in her chest when she heard the knock at the front door later that evening. She paused in the action of cutting some bananas for a fruit salad. His stance wary, Ryan's eyes flashed as he glanced at her.

"It's okay. If it's Marc, I want to talk to him," Mari told her brother with a reassuring smile. She felt her brother's stare on her as she walked out of the kitchen.

She opened the screen door. "Hi," she said tremulously. Marc stood there on the porch looking beautiful to her, his dark blond hair wind-ruffled, his jaw darkened with whiskers, his blue eyes gleaming in his shadowed face.

"Hi."

A ripple of sensation coursed down her neck and spine at the sound of his low, hoarse voice.

He waved toward his car in the sunlit driveway. "Will you come for a ride?"

Mari nodded. She stepped out onto the porch, feeling like a prisoner walking to the gallows.

Neither of them spoke after they'd gotten into the car. Marc drove to The Family Center. He glanced over to her and gave a small smile when she gasped in pleasure. A painted blue, brown and ivory sign had been placed next to the entrance.

"I hope you don't mind," Marc said as he parked the car and nodded toward the freshly painted sign. "Liam had to get back to work, but when he heard about the Center, he wanted to do something. He commissioned Joe Brown to make it before he left Harbor Town. Joe left him a message saying he installed it Saturday."

Mari was too amazed to speak. They got out of the car and went to examine the sign. Joe had included a small landscape in the corner of the sign, a dune and a sunset. Mari recognized the vista off Silver Dune. Beneath the name of the organization and contact information, a two-word quote had been added.

"Choose hope," she whispered. After several seconds, she glanced up at Marc. He watched her, his eyes like two steady beacons beckoning her to shore. Her throat ached when she swallowed. "I need to make sure I get Liam's number from you. This was so wonderful of him."

Marc nodded and grabbed her hand. They took a rough path through evergreen, oak and maple until the tree line broke and they walked out onto the dune. Lake Michigan looked periwinkle blue beneath the fiery orange, sinking sun. When they reached the end of the dune, Mari turned toward him. She nodded toward the water in the vicinity of where they'd sat in the boat and watched the sun rising several days ago.

"We're back on the shore now," she said quietly. "Watching the sunset again."

His hand came up to cradle her jaw. He whisked his thumb across her cheek. "Sunrise. Sunset. They're all good, as long as you're here."

Mari distantly wondered if her throat would ever stop aching. Lately it seemed to be constantly swelling with emotion. "It's been a difficult trip...coming back to Harbor Town," she murmured.

"Mari, about what Colleen said in the hospital...I know it upset you. But Colleen was worried—"

"I know," Mari said rapidly. She turned toward the lake, missing Marc's caress when her motion caused his hand to fall away. "Of course she was upset. I would have been, too, given the circumstances. It's completely natural."

Out of the corner of her vision, she saw Marc stiffen.

"So why have you been avoiding me for the past few days?"

"I needed to think," Mari said, her gaze on the dancing waves of the silver-blue lake.

He didn't speak for several seconds. When she glanced over at him, she saw his mouth had drawn into a straight line. She'd never seen Marc look so grim. Somehow he'd guessed what she was about to say.

"Don't do this, Mari."

"One of us has to," she said in a hushed voice. "I was right. It would never work, you and me."

"It *does* work," he said, putting his hand on her upper arm. "It always has!"

"For us," Mari replied, just as heatedly. "It works for *us,* Marc. But we're not the only two people on the planet. There are other people…other lives we have to take into account."

"I don't accept that. We're not hurting anyone by being together. What happened with my mother was scary for everyone, but that had nothing to do with you starting The Family Center or us being together. It had *everything* to do with the fact that she's been ignoring her physical health. I've had a long conversation with her about it. She's agreed to take her medication now and follow the doctor's treatment advice."

"I spoke with Brigit, as well."

He paused for two heartbeats. "You did? About what?" he asked warily.

"She seems to be of the opinion that you want me this much because I was the one thing you never could have."

"And you believed her?" Marc asked, anger entering his tone.

"No…at least not totally."

"What's that supposed to mean? *Not totally?*"

She paused for a moment, gathering herself. She waved toward the edge of the dune in the distance.

"Do you remember us standing there on the end of this dune together? It would have been fifteen summers ago. Just weeks before the crash, if I'm not mistaken."

He didn't respond to her quiet question, but she sensed the tension coiling in his muscles.

"I was terrified," she said softly. "Literally. I still have a fear of heights, you know. But I jumped. Do you know why?"

She turned to look at him, but he still didn't speak. She hated seeing the rigid, hard lines of his face cast in the crimson rays of the dying sun. His eyes were usually so alive when he looked at her, but at that moment, they looked cold with dread.

"Because, once upon a time, I would have followed Marc Kavanaugh anywhere. *Anywhere,*" she added fervently. She shook her head sadly. "But things changed. And I'm not a child anymore. I have others to consider."

"I see. We're back to this, then. I'm the selfish one, for suggesting we should be together."

Mari closed her eyes and felt tears skitter down her cheek. The wind increased and tossed the trees behind them. The waves hitting the sand beach in the distance sounded lonely. She pushed her blowing hair off her damp face.

"I don't think that anymore. You're not selfish. You're strong. Stronger than I am. You said you would accept my decision after we returned from Chicago." She swallowed convulsively. "Please understand. I'm not strong enough to follow you this time around."

She turned away from the lake and paused. "Ryan and I booked flights back home. We leave tomorrow. I can finish what remains to be done for The Family

Center from there. I'll go inside now and tie up a few loose ends. Ryan can pick me up here later." She lowered her head, praying for strength to continue. "There's... there's something I'll need to speak with you about, but...perhaps it'd be best if it waited until I was in San Francisco."

She glanced up at him. This was by far the hardest thing she'd ever done. Her entire body hurt as if every cell protested at the idea of leaving him. She touched her stomach in an instinctive protective gesture. *This* life was the one that had decided her, in the end. She needed to protect her child from the pain and heartache of their past. Wasn't fate screaming loud and clear that they weren't meant to be together? How many more people would be hurt if they tried?

"Good-bye," she said quietly.

He said nothing, but she felt his gaze on her as she walked back through the trees alone.

Chapter Fourteen

Six weeks later, Ryan and Mari paused by the front door of her condominium. She knew what her brother was going to say before he said it.

"You're not yourself, Mari. I'm worried about you."

"I'm *fine*. You were at the doctor's appointment with me two days ago. You heard it yourself. I couldn't be healthier and neither could the baby."

Ryan looked doubtful. She knew he'd been referring to her spirits, not her physical well-being. Before he could say anything else, she kissed him farewell on the jaw.

"I'll talk to you soon?"

Ryan opened his mouth and then closed it again. "Yeah. Okay. Call me if you need me," he said with a pointed glance before he walked out the door.

Ever since she'd broken the news to Ryan about her pregnancy two weeks ago, he was constantly dropping by and checking her pantry to see if she had enough food, or lecturing her about little things, like when he noticed she'd used a small ladder to change a lightbulb.

She sighed and picked up the bag of items he'd dropped off and carried them to her dining room. Ryan meant well. He was as hyperaware as she was that her baby's father wasn't around to look out for her. When she'd told him who the father was, it had not been a comfortable moment.

Since then, neither of them had mentioned Marc's name out loud.

She still hadn't called Marc to break the news. It just seemed too overwhelming. Insurmountable, in fact. She couldn't seem to build up the energy required to tell Marc they were going to have a baby, if not a future, together.

She set the bag of items on her dining room table with a thud, purposefully trying to scatter her thoughts of Marc. She kept waiting for the pain to fade, but after being in San Francisco for six weeks now, it still hurt to think of him…to recall his face as they stood together on Silver Dune.

She'd kept herself busy with her symphony work and making plans for the baby's nursery. She'd turned over much of the day-to-day preparations for The Family Center to Allison Trainor, Eric Reyes and Colleen. Constantly conversing with the Harbor Town residents—especially Colleen—had made her too depressed. She'd needed to cut back on her interactions for basic survival's sake.

Of course limiting her communications with Eric or Colleen hadn't stopped her from waking up in the middle of the night in a state of panic, feeling as if she'd left something crucial behind. The dreams varied, but the experience of waking in a cold sweat, anxiety clawing at her throat was the same. That, and the inevitable tears that followed.

The experience was very similar to what had occurred when she'd been uprooted and moved to San Francisco fifteen years ago.

It was so hard to keep reminding herself she was doing the right thing when it felt so wrong.

Mari opened the green garbage bag on the table and withdrew a smaller, sealed bag filled with photos. She took out a black-and-white one and smiled at the handsome couple posing for their wedding picture.

"That's your grandma and grandpa," Mari whispered, her hand on her belly.

She definitely possessed a small baby bump now, something that was only identifiable to Mari and a few people who were in the know. She'd taken to talking to the baby, much to her own amusement.

"They would have spoiled you rotten, especially my dad," she told the baby.

She reached into the plastic bag and pulled out a black yearbook. All of the items had come from the Harbor Town basement. The house had sold three weeks ago. Ryan had brought back the remaining family items when he returned to San Francisco. He'd just recently divided them up, however, and brought Mari's share to her condominium tonight. Or at least that's the reason he'd given for dropping by on a Friday night at eight o'clock. Mari knew it really was just an excuse for checking up on her.

Who knew her big, bad, fighter pilot brother could be such a mother hen?

Mari checked the year on the book and saw that it was her own yearbook from her senior year. She'd been seventeen years old, filled with hope and head over heels in love with Marc. It'd been torture for her to be separated from him during the fall, winter and spring, although he would drive up to Dearborn occasionally. His visits had always been short, though, given her parents' disapproval of their relationship.

She opened up the yearbook, smiling wistfully when she recognized youthful, long-forgotten faces.

It was cruel, the way time fell through your grasping fingers.

She paused when she saw a light pink envelope inserted between some pages. She opened up the envelope and realized it was her graduation card from her parents. Below the printed inscription, she saw both her parents' handwriting.

From her mother: *We will always be proud of our beautiful daughter. Always. Congratulations, Marianna!*

She blinked a few unwanted tears out of her eyes so that she could see her father's note.

Mari, Your entire future stretches ahead of you. My advice to you as you set about your journey is to never give up hope. Hope is putting faith to work when doubting would be easier. Know that you will always have our love, Dad.

For a full minute, she just stood there, staring at the message. It was as if she'd just looked up and seen Kassim Itani standing there…saw his thin face and small smile and the knowing twinkle in his dark eyes. The years had collapsed.

Her father had reached out and touched her across the vast barrier of time.

Still holding the card, she walked over to the window and stared out at the glittering high-rises, not really seeing them, but instead seeing her father's face…

And Marc's.

Hope is putting faith to work when doubting would be easier.

That's what she'd done. She'd doubted when she should have hung on. She'd done the wise thing, the rational thing, but everyone knew hope wasn't logical.

"Choose hope."

It took her a moment to realize she wasn't speaking to the baby. She was whispering to herself.

"Your mother is here, Marc."

He did a double take at his administrative assistant's unexpected announcement.

"Where?"

Adrian pointed at the office assigned to him at the courthouse at 26th and California. He had a briefing to attend with some of his top attorneys who were prosecuting a police officer accused of murdering his wife. It was a high profile case and he needed to do a million things before the briefing. All of those things faded in his mind at the news his mother was in his office. Brigit rarely came to the city, let alone to the criminal courthouse.

"Thanks, Adrian," Marc muttered before he plunged into his office. His mother stood from her chair and turned to him. Marc thought she looked healthy enough, but—"

"Is everything all right, Mom?"

"Everything's fine."

Marc gave her a quizzical glance as he deposited his heavy briefcase on his desk. "Why are you here, then?" he asked, bending to give her a kiss.

"I just wanted to speak to you."

"About what?" Marc asked as he settled in his chair.

Brigit also sat. "I was worried. You seemed so distant when we spoke on the phone yesterday."

"I'm fine."

"You're missing Mari."

He blinked, shocked his mother had just said a name that was typically *verboten* to her. It was all the more disorienting to hear Mari's name because he himself hadn't spoken it since she'd left Harbor Town six weeks ago. He said it in his mind frequently enough. Too often, in fact.

"What makes you say that?" he asked, once he'd re-covered from the shock of his mother willfully bringing up the topic of Mari Itani.

"Because I know you. It's killing you that she left."

Marc didn't reply, just flipped the pen he'd been twiddling in his fingers onto the desk. He was getting angry.

"What's your point, Mom? You came all the way to Chicago to say I've been missing Mari? So what if I have been?"

Brigit pursed her lips together before she spoke. "I thought perhaps I might be able to ease your misery some."

His laugh was harsh. "I doubt it."

Brigit inhaled deeply and then plunged ahead. "Per-haps. Perhaps not. I wanted to tell you that a week or two after Mari returned to Harbor Town—two days after my heart attack, in fact—I saw Mari at Harbor Town Memorial. She'd had an appointment there."

Marc's brown wrinkled in consternation. "Yeah. She hadn't been feeling well."

"Those dizzy spells. And nausea, perhaps?" Brigit asked.

"What are you getting at?"

"She was coming out of an obstetrician's office, Marc. She told me herself she'd had an appointment there."

He just stared at his mother's face. In the distance a car alarm started blaring loudly.

"I've had my share of children. I know I haven't seen Mari for years, but there's a certain air a woman gets. There are signs. Mari is pregnant, Marc."

He continued to gape at his mother. His heartbeat started to throb uncomfortably loud in his ears.

Brigit cleared her throat. "And I don't think I need to tell you that if she was pregnant, it wasn't with your child."

"What?" he muttered. He felt like he was trying to absorb his mom's words and meaning through a thick layer of insulation.

"Even if you two had…intimate relations once Mari had come back to Harbor Town, she wouldn't have thought she was pregnant after a week. If she is pregnant—or even if she just *thought* so—it couldn't be with your child. Mari must have been involved with someone else, Marc. That's why I came to Chicago. I thought it might ease the sting of her leaving some…to know she must have been involved with another man."

Marc sat forward slowly in his chair. "That's why you came here? To tell me that…you thought it would make me feel *better?*" When his mother didn't respond, Marc dazedly shook his head. "That's one hell of a mean-spirited thing to do, Mom."

Brigit's face collapsed. "I'm doing it for you, Marc."

"No," he stated harshly. "You're doing it for yourself. You're doing it because you want the threat of Mari to disappear for good." He stood abruptly, causing Brigit to start. He reached for his briefcase. "The incredible thing about it is, you did the opposite."

Brigit stood, looking flustered. "What do you mean? Where are you going?"

"I'm going after Mari."

He didn't look back at his mother as he stormed out of the office.

He called to book a flight while he was in the cab. He didn't even bother to go back to his condo to pack anything. This was too important. He was halfway to the airport and apologizing to an assistant district attorney for not being able to attend the upcoming briefing when another call came through on his cell.

He did a double take when he saw the caller identification.

It was Mari.

Why the hell was she calling him now when she'd refused all of his calls since she'd left?

He so forcefully plunged through the revolving doors of the Palmer House Hotel that they kept spinning a full revolution once he was inside. Mari looked over her shoulder at the sound, her eyes huge in her face. For a second he just stood there, dazed.

Mari's eyes. God, would he ever get over their impact?

She turned around. Everything seemed to slow down around him. Sounds became muffled and distant. It was just like when he'd followed her from her concert and walked through these very doors. She'd turned and he'd been compelled to call out when he'd seen her exquisite face.

This time was the same…and it was a thousand times different.

His gaze skimmed over her. She looked incomparably beautiful to him, wearing a dark blue skirt and a soft, cream-colored knit top that clung to her breasts. His eyes rested on the curve of her belly. He met her stare.

"Three months," she said quietly.

"Why didn't you tell me?" he whispered.

Her smile practically undid him. She stepped closer.

"I wanted to tell you about the baby. More than

anything. But I had myself convinced I was doing the right thing by staying away. It took a voice from the past to make me see I wasn't being wise. I was just giving into my fear…my doubts about the future. Our future. I made that realization last night, Marc, and I got on the first plane here this morning. I hope you can forgive me—"

Her words were cut off when he reached for her and lifted her in his arms. He buried his face in the soft fabric of her sweater and inhaled her scent.

"You're sure? You're not going to leave again?" he asked in a garbled voice.

She was pressing small, frantic kisses against his neck and jaw. He felt the wetness of her tears on his skin. "No. Never again."

"You'll stay with me?"

She put her hands on each side of his head and looked into his eyes. "I promise. If that's what you want. I wasn't sure…those things you said about not wanting another relationship—"

"Did you actually think that applies when it comes to *you?*" he asked incredulously. He kissed her with the single intent of silencing her doubts on that front.

"Our future was ripped away from us so long ago," Mari murmured when he lifted his head a moment later. "We've been given a second chance. It's a blessing, and I'm so sorry I couldn't see that before."

"As long as you see it now," he whispered, his mouth hovering next to her lips. He kissed her softly, and when he caught her taste, hungrily. He growled low in his throat before he lifted his head. "God, I love you so much. I can't believe we're going to have a baby."

She smiled. "I love you, too."

He kissed away the tears on her cheek. "The future starts now, Mari."

She took his hand and placed it on the curve of her belly. He went still at the sensation.

"Actually it started twelve or so weeks ago." Her golden brown eyes were filled with joy and amusement as she glanced up at the high-ceilinged lobby. "Right in this very place."

He smiled slowly. Laughter burst out of her throat when he spun her around, her long hair flying in the air. He set her back down on her feet and leaned over her. He spoke to her through nibbling kisses on her lips.

"What do you say we go back up to your room and celebrate our future to its fullest?"

She leaned up and pressed her mouth to his. He held her tight. Marc had the vague, distant impression that they were attracting a few stares from passersby, but he couldn't have cared less. The realization had struck him that he held his whole world in his arms.

His future...*their* future had never shone so bright.

Epilogue

The following spring

Mari thought her heart would burst with joy. The child in her arms had never seemed so beautiful to her as she did at that moment, nor had the man who sat beside her looked so wonderful. She squeezed Marc's hand. He turned to her and smiled.

Perhaps it was the sublime spring day or maybe it was the special event they attended. The priest solemnly continued with his blessing of the lovely memorial fountain Marc had had commissioned to be built at the edge of the woods on Silver Dune.

She glanced down the row of seated visitors and caught sight of Eric Reyes. She smiled when he gave her a quick thumb's up. She was sorry to see that Natalie hadn't been tempted out of her solitude to attend the lovely outdoor ceremony.

Rylee Jean Kavanaugh chose that moment to make a

loud, burbling sound in her sleep. Marc and she glanced down in surprise and concern, but Rylee resumed her peaceful nap, her tiny, rose-colored lips making a rhythmic, pursing movement as she slept.

"She's going to wake up hungry as a horse," Marc whispered.

Mari noticed his devilish grin and the way his gleaming blue eyes flickered quickly over her breasts.

"She's got an appetite like you," Mari whispered back, giving him a mock look of censorship.

Something caught her eye at the back of the seating area. Her smile faded. Marc turned to look where she stared.

"I can't believe she came," she whispered.

They watched Colleen Kavanaugh lead her mother to a seat in the back row. Almost every seat they'd set up in the clearing had been taken. The Family Center had gotten off to an excellent start. Clients attended the ceremony, as did family members, employees and people from the town.

Father Mike continued. "We would like to end this ceremony by having each of you bless this fountain. Those who have survived the pains of substance abuse and those who are trying to find the hope within themselves in order to survive please come to the front, grab a small portion of salt and toss it into the fountain. The salt represents toil and tears, but also stands for hope. Hope is invisible, something we must find within ourselves using the vision not of our eyes but of faith. Your blessings and wishes today may disappear like the salt in the water, but this fountain will be replenished and strengthened by your hope for the future. Please come forward and cast your wishes into this fountain."

People began to stand and join in a line. Mari glanced back halfway through the ceremony and saw Brigit

Kavanaugh sitting next to her daughter. She looked stiff and uncomfortable, as if she'd gate-crashed a party where she wasn't welcome.

Things had improved between Brigit and Mari since she had moved to Chicago, obtained a position with the Chicago Symphony Orchestra and married Marc. Rylee had been born four-and-a-half weeks ago, and a granddaughter had certainly made Brigit warmer, at times reminding Mari of the woman she used to know. However, Brigit still became tight-mouthed when any mention of The Family Center was made. That was why Mari was shocked Colleen had persuaded her mother to come.

Mari glanced uncertainly at Marc as they came back from dropping their salt into the fountain. He gave her a small smile of encouragement, and her love for him swelled. He'd been so supportive of everything she'd done with The Family Center. She knew he felt bad that his mother kept up a silent opposition to the project.

Father Mike said a few closing words and a prayer, and everyone started to depart. There was a reception following the ceremony in The Family Center. Mari should get inside there to help.

Instead, she stood. "I'll be right back," she whispered to Marc.

Brigit and Colleen were standing in preparation to leave when Mari approached. She still held a sleeping Rylee in one arm, but she extended her other hand.

"Brigit," she said softly.

Brigit seemed confused, but she hesitantly took Mari's hand.

She led her mother-in-law to the podium that stood in the front. Everyone was milling about or departing, their attention elsewhere, but she sensed Marc's gaze on her like a reassuring touch. She nodded at the gold bowl containing the salt.

"Take some, Brigit."

Brigit stiffened at her words.

"This ceremony is for the survivors of substance abuse," Mari spoke quietly. "That's what you are, Brigit. That's what this place is about. It's about making a future despite the pain of the past."

She saw Brigit's throat convulse. For a second, Mari worried she was going to turn and walk away, but then Brigit reached with a trembling hand. Mari gave her a smile and led her to the edge of the lovely, new, stone-and-metal fountain.

Brigit held out her arm. The grains fell through her parted fingers like solidified tears. The hand that had released the salt found Mari's. Mari felt Brigit's flesh shaking next to her own. She tightly clasped Brigit's hand before they turned away.

Mari and Marc stood in each other's arms later. They stared out at the lake and the sinking sun. Almost everyone had left the reception at The Family Center. Marc had asked her to take a walk with him, and Colleen had happily agreed to watch her niece for a few minutes.

"Every time I think I couldn't love you more you prove me wrong," Marc said quietly from above her.

"I feel the same way about you."

He grinned and lowered his head, nuzzling her nose. "I'm thankful you decided to take the leap, Mari."

"It's only half as scary with you next to me."

"And twice as exciting."

"Cocky," she chastised softly. She went up on her toes and kissed her husband in the golden light of the setting sun.

* * * * *

*Look for Liam Kavanaugh's story,
coming soon to Special Edition.*

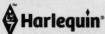
Harlequin®

COMING NEXT MONTH

Available April 26, 2011

SPECIAL EDITION

REQUEST YOUR FREE BOOKS!

2 FREE NOVELS PLUS 2 FREE GIFTS!

SPECIAL EDITION

Life, Love & Family

YES! Please send me 2 FREE Harlequin Special Edition® novels and my 2 FREE gifts (gifts are worth about $10). After receiving them, if I don't wish to receive any more books, I can return the shipping statement marked "cancel." If I don't cancel, I will receive 6 brand-new novels every month and be billed just $4.24 per book in the U.S. or $4.99 per book in Canada. That's a saving of at least 15% off the cover price! It's quite a bargain! Shipping and handling is just 50¢ per book in the U.S. and 75¢ per book in Canada.* I understand that accepting the 2 free books and gifts places me under no obligation to buy anything. I can always return a shipment and cancel at any time. Even if I never buy another book, the two free books and gifts are mine to keep forever.

235/335 SDN FC7H

Name _____ (PLEASE PRINT) _____

Address _____ Apt. # _____

City _____ State/Prov. _____ Zip/Postal Code _____

Signature (if under 18, a parent or guardian must sign) _____

Mail to the **Reader Service:**
IN U.S.A.: P.O. Box 1867, Buffalo, NY 14240-1867
IN CANADA: P.O. Box 609, Fort Erie, Ontario L2A 5X3

Not valid for current subscribers to Harlequin Special Edition books.

Want to try two free books from another line?
Call 1-800-873-8635 or visit www.ReaderService.com.

* Terms and prices subject to change without notice. Prices do not include applicable taxes. Sales tax applicable in N.Y. Canadian residents will be charged applicable taxes. Offer not valid in Quebec. This offer is limited to one order per household. All orders subject to credit approval. Credit or debit balances in a customer's account(s) may be offset by any other outstanding balance owed by or to the customer. Please allow 4 to 6 weeks for delivery. Offer available while quantities last.

Your Privacy—The Reader Service is committed to protecting your privacy. Our Privacy Policy is available online at www.ReaderService.com or upon request from the Reader Service.

We make a portion of our mailing list available to reputable third parties that offer products we believe may interest you. If you prefer that we not exchange your name with third parties, or if you wish to clarify or modify your communication preferences, please visit us at www.ReaderService.com/consumerchoice or write to us at Reader Service Preference Service, P.O. Box 9062, Buffalo, NY 14269. Include your complete name and address.

HSE11

With an evil force hell-bent on destruction, two enemies must unite to find a truth that turns all-too-personal when passions collide.

Enjoy a sneak peek in Jenna Kernan's next installment in her original TRACKER *series, GHOST STALKER, available in May, only from Harlequin Nocturne.*

"**W**ho are you?" he snarled.

Jessie lifted her chin. "Your better."

His smile was cold. "Such arrogance could only come from a Niyanoka."

She nodded. "Why are you here?"

"I don't know." He glanced about her room. "I asked the birds to take me to a healer."

"And they have done so. Is that *all* you asked?"

"No. To lead them away from my friends." His eyes fluttered and she saw them roll over white.

Jessie straightened, preparing to flee, but he roused himself and mastered the momentary weakness. His eyes snapped open, locking on her.

Her heart hammered as she inched back.

"Lead who away?" she whispered, suddenly afraid of the answer.

"The ghosts. Nagi sent them to attack me so I would bring them to her."

The wolf must be deranged because Nagi did not send ghosts to attack living creatures. He captured the evil ones after their death if they refused to walk the Way of Souls, forcing them to face judgment.

"Her? The healer you seek is also female?"

"Michaela. She's Niyanoka, like you. The last Seer of Souls and Nagi wants her dead."

Jessie fell back to her seat on the carpet as the possibility of this ricocheted in her brain. Could it be true?

"Why should I believe you?" But she knew why. His black aura, the part that said he had been touched by death. Only a ghost could do that. But it made no sense.

Why would Nagi hunt one of her people and why would a Skinwalker want to protect her? She had been trained from birth to hate the Skinwalkers, to consider them a threat.

His intent blue eyes pinned her. Jessie felt her mouth go dry as she considered the impossible. Could the trickster be speaking the truth? Great Mystery, what evil was this?

She stared in astonishment. There was only one way to find her answers. But she had never even met a Skinwalker before and so did not even know if they dreamed.

But if he dreamed, she would have her chance to learn the truth.

*Look for GHOST STALKER by Jenna Kernan,
available May only from Harlequin Nocturne,
wherever books and ebooks are sold.*

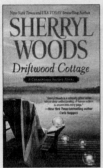
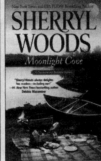